GRAND PORTAGE INCIDENT

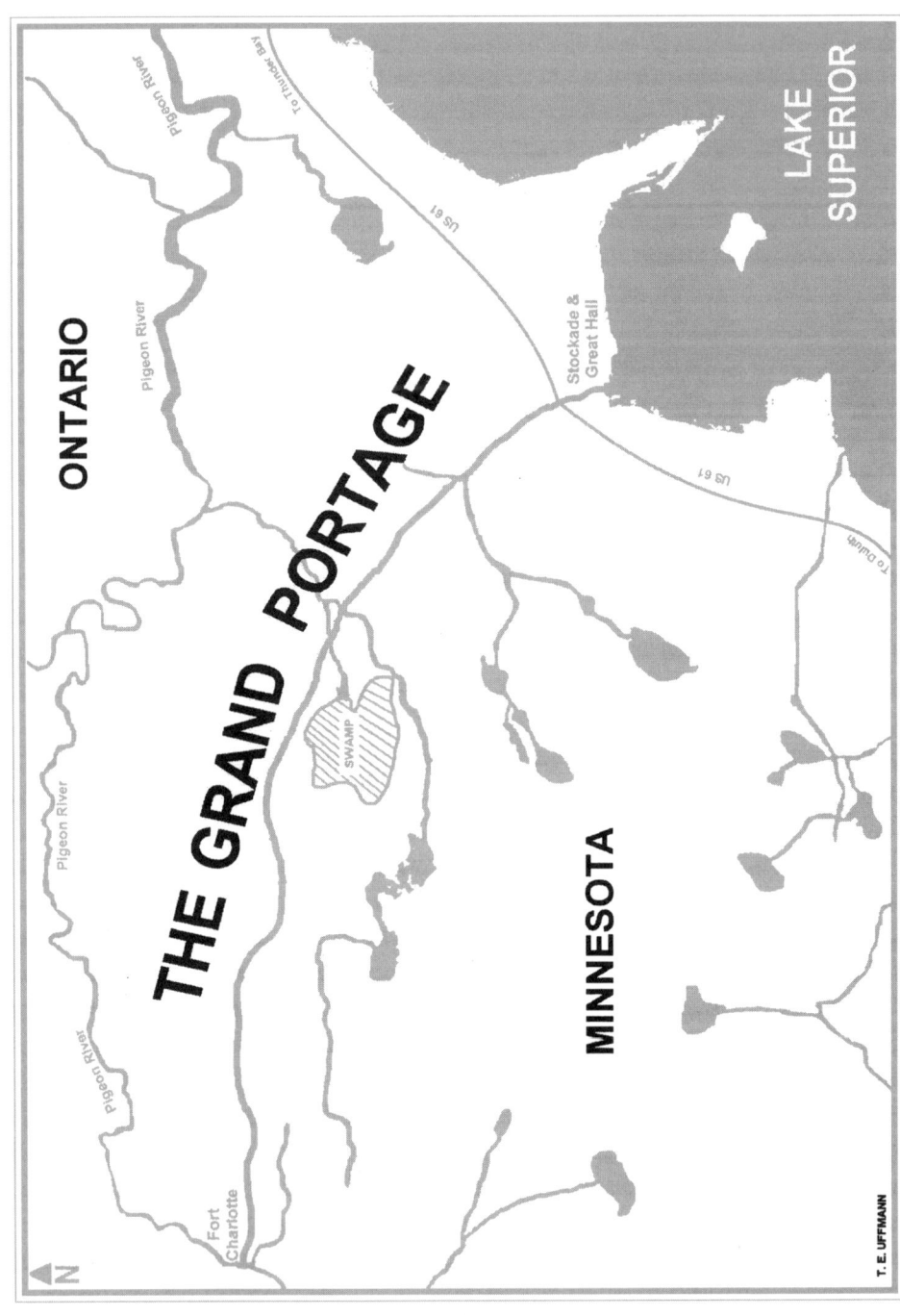

A NOVEL

GRAND PORTAGE INCIDENT

By
Gene Andereck

Shawnee Mission, Kansas

All characters in this novel are fictional. Any resemblance to persons living or dead is purely coincidental. Events in the story also are fictitious.

"Early Life," a poem from The Black Hawk Songs, by Michael Borich, Springfield, Missouri, is reprinted with the author's permission.

The map was produced by Tom Uffmann, Springfield, Missouri.

Copyright © 2000 by Rock Creek Press, L.L.C.

All rights reserved, including the right of reproduction in whole or in part in any form.

Published by Rock Creek Press, L.L.C., 10167 Haskins St., Shawnee Mission, Kansas 66215-1857

Andereck, Gene
   Grand Portage Incident

ISBN: 1-890826-05-7

Printed in the United States of America
First Edition: September 2000

1098765432

TO

Alison
Leslie
Lauren
Nels
Jack

Early Life

My ways
of deadfall and rope snare traps,

bow-drill firemaking, beaming
and fleshing a hide, weaving
basswood bark, ribbing a canoe

and arrow fletching filled my
learning days. From the mighty
water straining at its banks

to the sloping limestone bluff
behind our village I grew wise
to beaver, mink and deer, rabbit

porcupine and the whispered
forest speech. Descending,
the beautiful woman from

the clouds shared venison
and through the spread veins
of her right hand brings forth

corn and beans. In the days of
my father's lodge I knew the habits
of my people, customs and laws

from *The Black Hawk Songs*
      by Michael Borich

TO THE READER

GRAND PORTAGE INCIDENT is the second book of my Arrowhead Trilogy. As with the first, TRIAL AT GRAND MARAIS, I renamed the Ojibwa Reservation to identify its general geographical location for Canadian and American readers who have never been to the Arrowhead Country. While I have used literary license to create the lava tubes described on the portage and set the traditional gathering of Chippewa from across the Midwest and Canada in the spring rather than fall, on the whole my descriptions are accurate.

For two hundred years the moccasins of thousands of French voyageurs trod Grand Portage at the Pigeon River boundary between the United States and Canada carrying trade goods and furs. The reader who wants to experience that nine-mile trek in the same unspoiled wilderness can do so today.

G.A.

CHAPTER ONE

A morning fog rolled into the side streets at the edge of the campus of the Fond Du Lac Community College. Like an old photo mottled by mildew, the buildings were veiled with a shadow of death. Death's presence showed on the pale, drawn faces of students gathered at the curbs. It showed in the anxiety of the householders who stood in early morning light on wooden porches and flat lawns hunched against damp air. Flashing lights reflected in the wet streets from the patrol cars, an ambulance, and a fire truck that converged on the women's dormitory.

The Indian tribe's unique multimillion dollar community college in Cloquet, Minnesota is a layout of multiple buildings designed to fit the architect's concept of a gigantic bear paw print. The buildings are constructed in round forms and one drum-shaped room has an archival library where documents of historical interest to Ojibwa people are collected and studied. The idea of the drum-shape – which communicates over long distances – symbolizes the communication of the information gathered in the library of the college.

The girls' dormitory was one of the toes on the giant paw print.

Hazy uniformed figures stood about the entrance to the college building. A medical team carried a chalk white stretcher inside but did not come out. After an interval, someone shut off the motor on the ambulance. All watched the pulsing monotony of the blinking lights as the moist air crept up the hill from the St. Louis River. The wet silence seemed to confirm the rumor that a body had been found.

"Was she raped?" a voice called from one of the porches.

"No. Somebody said she found a man in her room going through her purse, and he killed her."

"They catch the guy?"

"They said they did."

A hundred miles up the lake, morning light reflected on the water at the side of a refurbished warehouse made into a combination apartment and law office. The structure was built on sturdy pilings in the harbor at Grand Marais, Minnesota. The smell of warming trees, pines and balsams, and resins beginning to soften on the south slope of the Sawtooth Mountains, gave the air its first real smell of spring.

Inside the apartment, a notion of aloneness penetrated the high ceiling rooms and stark furnishings. Each morning the feeling was the same when lawyer Errol Joyce arose. Joyce had never married. He had had a succession of special relationships, but the women he counted as special resented the law. They referred to the profession he loved as his jealous mistress.

Jan Kiel, the engaging State's attorney, had been the lone exception. Jan understood Joyce's single-minded devotion. However, now Jan, too, had stepped out of his personal life. Their affair had ended with a bitter quarrel. The clash left for them only a professional relationship, which they confined to their offices and the courtrooms. Others on the North Shore, who had speculated that the lawyer couple would marry, were confounded.

Lawyer Joyce stood on the balcony of his apartment, breathing in the changing of the season. He was anxious to get up on the Sawtooth Range to get the feel of the wilderness country at the breakup, to know once more the joy of a paddle in his hands and a canoe slipping along the shore. He wanted to dig his boots into the muskeg and feel the hard granite after months of skis, snowshoes, and white trails of the long winter. On the eaves of the building, he saw a squirrel sunning itself just above him. Its eyes were closed, but Joyce knew it was aware of his slightest move, for when the lawyer shifted his position, the white-edged rims opened wide. It stretched itself luxuriously, quivered in a sort of a squirrelly ecstasy, and loosened up as though it was undoing all the kinks and knots of winter from its muscles.

The City of Duluth and the fishing village of Grand Marais sit on a rock foundation that extends north and west from the shore of Lake Superior into the upper Midwest and central Canada. The border, an intricate tangle of paths, lakes, and rivers on the vast geological shield, separates the two countries. Mutual restrictions adopted by the United States and Canada ban commercial operations, machines, airplanes, and motors from the unspoiled area. Seven million acres of primitive lands are within the boundaries of Ontario's Quetico Provincial Park and Minnesota's Superior National Forest. For hundreds of years, before white fur traders arrived, the land was occupied by the Menominee, the Forest Sioux, and bands of Chippewa.

Through the open sliding door the lawyer's attention was

drawn to the words of a police officer being interviewed on his television set.

"She was found in a dormitory bed," said the officer.

"Can you confirm the victim's identity?" he was asked.

"Not at this time." The response was cautious.

"Students have identified the victim as being Zona Saulturs, an Indian girl from up on the Thunder Bay Reservation. Does that identification agree with the evidence the police have found?"

The officer shook his head. "We can't speculate as to the identity of the victim. The victim's face and hands have been badly disfigured with some kind of chemical."

"What was she wearing?"

"A wedding band."

"That's all? No clothing?"

"Yes," replied the officer.

Errol Joyce leaned back against the balcony railing. Behind him, foaming surf rolled in off the lake past the lighthouse and surged across the bay onto the rock shore beneath. The disposition of rubble and talus from off the mountain range that formed the North Shore of Lake Superior was in water too deep to let the waves grind them to sand. Over the deep waters of the bay, the waves rolled forward with an oscillating movement, but not enough to do anything more than reduce the rubble to a smoothly rounded form.

Errol could see the man on the picture tube was uncomfortable in the glare of the television camera. The officer tried to politely disengage himself from the reporter and her camera, but the interviewer again stepped in the man's path.

"The college security guard who arrived first is quoted as saying the police believe the victim was killed somewhere else and that her body was brought to the dormitory because you found no blood and little of the acid chemical on the bed sheets. Is that correct?"

"I have no comment on that."

"Is it true that the clotting of the blood has caused you to believe that the victim was dead for several hours before the acid was applied to her face?"

"I have no comment on that," the officer repeated.

"Was the acid forced down the girl's throat?" called the reporter. The officer disappeared out of camera range without answering. The reporter and her microphone turned and the picture grew until the woman's face filled Joyce's television screen.

"It is this reporter's information that the victim in fact is the community college student, Zona Saulturs, whose home is on the Thunder Bay Indian Reservation. She and her twin sister, Nina, are Native Americans and roommates living in the college dormitory. A student, who has not yet been identified, found the body and called the campus security. They in turn notified the police department. There is no information as to the whereabouts of the twin sister. We are told by a source close to the investigation that the victim's sister, Nina Saulturs, is thought by the police to have fled or to have been abducted because she is missing, as are select pieces of her wardrobe, her purse, and a suitcase. The automobile owned by the girls, a Honda Civic, is also missing."

Jan Kiel, Assistant Attorney General for the State of Minnesota, carefully stepped out of the tile shower. She set her wet feet flat on the paper floor mat that bore the logo, "Harbor Inn Motel and Lounge, Grand Marais, Minnesota." The words were stenciled alongside a picture of a leaping rainbow trout. She closed the dripping shower door, reached for a fluffy towel, and brushed hair back from her eyes. Jan draped the towel over her shoulders where it hung like a thick bedspread to her thighs and back of her long legs. Using a second towel, she dried while she examined herself in the mirrored wall.

Except at her nipples, the young woman's body was without blemish, smooth and round like a melon. Her face was set with sunken shadows at the cheekbones, which were plastered with fine, wet strands of yellow hair.

The woman lawyer smiled at the reflection. Her breasts were swollen. When she pressed them, the veins showed purple streaks at the nipples and caused tender sensations, but less painful than during her first month. Jan slowly turned and examined herself holding a hand mirror to see drops of water glistening on her flattened backside. The weight, she noticed, was now forward and lower. She finished toweling and hung up the damp cloth. The anticipation put points of light in her eyes. She closed her eyelids and stroked the wondrous miracle inside her. Tenderly she slid the damp palms of her hands down each side of her belly and inhaled a deep breath.

"This thirty-second year is going to be the most exciting year of my life."

She said aloud the words as if to reinforce her belief that the statement was true.

"In perfect health," Dr. Erickson had said. Jan was certain he was right. She felt so much different, better, than she had the afternoon in the Duluth hospital when she and Errol Joyce had their bitter argument.

Again addressing the mirror, she said aloud, "And I am not going to put his name on the birth certificate."

Jan had taken the precaution to have two doctors.

Dr. Johanna Baker, Obstetrician, practiced in Duluth where the lawyer had her home and office. Dr. Jens Erickson, her other choice, practiced in Grand Marais. Jan knew that most of her last trimester would be spent arguing cases in the Cook County District Court, one hundred miles up Superior's North Shore. Consequently she arranged for a duplicate of her medical records to be kept at the Grand Marais Memorial Hospital. Her two physicians had no trouble in accommodating. They even wagered as to who would do the delivery. Whether Dr. Erickson or her Duluth obstetrician won the wager depended on which doctor was closest when she went into labor.

"I am pregnant, not ill," Jan had insisted when she announced her intention to try every case on her trial schedule until the hour she delivered. District Court Judge Dorothy Clemens agreed and accommodated the young lawyer by calling frequent recesses early on in Jan's trials when the State's attorney had experienced bouts of nausea.

In her seventh month, as spring arrived and as she had expected, the lawyer divided time between her office in Duluth and the courthouse in Grand Marais.

Jan opened her eyes and stared at the image in the mirror.

Her work in the courtrooms on the Iron Range brought her into frequent contact with Errol Joyce. Of late, each encounter ended with intemperate words.

"It has been easier without him," she insisted, again speaking aloud to confirm the thought. When she spoke she felt surfacing of the bitterness that had flooded between her and the man who fathered her child.

Slowly Jan turned from the mirror.

"There is no excuse, absolutely no excuse," she thought, "for a man to want to harm his own baby." She resolved that the name of the father would remain a blank when she registered the birth. Errol was fifteen years her senior. "No wonder he did not understand," she thought. Jan would never deny that she loved her baby's father, but she would not put his name on the birth certificate.

She turned again to the mirror and spoke to the reflection. "When my baby is old enough to understand, I will explain."

The telephone beside the bed rang.

The early morning promise of a clearing sky was frustrated by a thick fog, which moved in from the lake. The bay was becoming heavy with mist. The lawyer wrapped the towel tightly above her breasts and tucked in a corner to free her hands. After first switching on the room's lights, Jan Kiel picked up the receiver.

"Yes?"

"This is Errol," said the familiar voice at the other end of the line.

The voice gave her pause.

Errol Joyce waited, then asked, "Jan? Are you there?"

"Yes. I am here." She willed herself to make her voice sound flat and unemotional. "What do you want?"

"Jan, I've got some bad news."

After another long pause, the woman said, "Errol it seems like of late you always have bad news."

"I didn't call to talk with you about our baby."

"I never thought that you did. What did you call to talk about?"

She heard the rush of words from the man at the other end of the telephone line. "Marie's daughter, Zona Saulturs, is dead! I just heard it on television."

The words gave Jan Kiel a stab of pain in her gut. "Oh my God!" She sank down on the bed. Her anger at Errol Joyce for the moment dissipated.

Errol continued. "They found Zona's body in bed in her dormitory. The guy that did it had poured acid on her face and hands."

"Oh, my God! How do they know it was a guy that did it?"

"They caught him a couple of blocks away from the campus. He had her credit cards and some of her jewelry in his pocket when they searched him."

"That son-of-a-bitch." Jan choked out the words.

"I'm sorry," Errol said. "I know how much she meant to you."

Tears began to roll down Jan Kiel's cheeks.

There was silence from the other end of the telephone line.

Jan looked out the hotel window. Across the gravel shore only a block away she could see Errol Joyce's apartment, which hung on the end of the warehouse. The roof lines showed the new addition had vaulted ceilings. Its glass walls and the redwood deck stuck out into the harbor. And, over the roof lines she could see the first haze of light green on the mountain above the town, the budding out of the aspen; the best of the tree's color before it begins to darken, while still misty and pastel.

"Zona!" Jan whispered the dead girl's name. "I was going to name my baby Zona. Zona Kiel."

Joyce thought Jan's remark was spoken to hurt him as much as to express feelings for the dead Indian girl. Her voice had a sharp edge that Errol Joyce did not miss.

There was silence on his end of the telephone line.

"What about her sister, Nina?" Jan finally asked.

"They don't know," Joyce's telephone voice answered flatly. "They say she ran off or was abducted. Some of her clothing and the car that their mother gave them is missing too."

"You say they caught the son-of-a-bitch who did it?" Jan's sorrow fogged her lawyer mind.

"That was on the news report."

The voice of the woman turned bitter. "I am going to call my boss and tell him I want in that case. The prosecuting attorney in St. Louis County is going to ask for help from the Attorney General's office and I want that assignment."

"Jan, you were too close to the twins. He will never assign that case to you. You have a personal interest in what has happened. You have no business prosecuting the guy they caught even if he is the one who did it. Besides," added Joyce, "if charges are filed and your boss did give you the assignment, the arraignment will come up next month which is getting pretty close to your due date."

"That is no longer any concern of yours, Errol."

"Dammit! Jan. It is my child too!"

"Not if I don't name you as the father on the birth certificate." She heard the sound of fierce breathing. Then a sharp click as the telephone receiver on the other end of the line was slammed down on its cradle.

In the living room of his apartment, Errol Joyce stared at

the telephone and muttered, "I shouldn't have done that, but sometimes she can be a real bitch!"

The lawyer was debating whether to call back and apologize for ending their conversation so rudely when the instrument started ringing. Her calling, he thought, but the voice at the other end of the line was not Jan Kiel.

"Errol?"

"Yes."

"This is Sam Applebee!"

"I know," the lawyer spoke abruptly. "What does the Black Bear want now?"

Joyce once testified before the Senate Committee on Indian Affairs that the Black Bear was a creature of the collective guilt of every white man in North America.

The Bear was a gambling house.

It was one of two casinos operated on reservation lands by the Fond Du Lac band of Chippewa Indians. The larger casino, Fond Du Luth, is located in the center of Duluth, Minnesota. The Black Bear, however, is located on Interstate Route 35 west of Duluth, a three-hour drive or a half-hour flight from the fishing village of Grand Marais.

At the time the tribe's reservation was established in 1854, it totaled 98,000 acres.

In exchange for the reservation acreage and an empty promise of food, clothing, and agricultural implements, the Lake bands put their mark on the Treaty of La Point and ceded most of the Arrowhead Country to the United States Government. The ceded land gave possession of all the timber and rich ore lands north and south of Lake Superior to the white man. Government surveyors cut off the rice and fish lakes south of the reservation lands, and after protests that the tribe could not survive without rice and fish, the Government added some of the area back, but cut off other acreage. Presently the Fond Du Lac Reservation trust area totals 22,000 acres. The tribe only owns 4,800 acres, which it never gave up to the white man. Since establishment of the reservation, the Government has permitted the Indians to lease 17,000 acres of allotted land, which they will lose if they do not keep up the allotment - lease payments.

Despite the tribe's hundred year effort to survive and improve its economy, Joyce had told the congressional committee that a third of the 6,000 tribe members were unemployed. Joyce knew first hand that to be a fact because for years he represented the Ojibwa bands. He had guided them through the government red tape to establish their hotels and casinos. And when casino revenues began to flow into the tribe's treasury, Joyce helped the Ojibwa School Board establish its unique community college where a horrible crime was committed.

Sam Applebee, short and round with the ruddy complexion of an early autumn apple, was an important man at the Black Bear Casino. He was one of the tribe's non Native American employees. As comptroller, he was caretaker of the money that bus loads of tourists left at the casino. Applebee had a Master's Degree from the Business Department of the University of Minnesota. The accountant was chief financial officer of the tribe and a close personal friend of Marie Saulturs, chief of the Ojibwa band on the Thunder Bay Reservation, which operated the Grand Portage Casino. Marie Saulturs relied on Applebee to run her tribe's business enterprises, as well as those of the Fond Du Lac band.

Sam Applebee was as highly regarded as their attorney, Errol Joyce, by most members of the Chippewa band. But Joyce didn't like Applebee and Sam Applebee made no pretense at liking Joyce.

"Errol, I need you as soon as you can fly down here."

"What's the problem?" Joyce asked.

"Can't say over the telephone. Someone is flying in from Las Vegas who wants to hire you."

"Strange," thought Joyce. Why hadn't the "someone flying in from Las Vegas" called him direct instead of having Applebee set up a meeting?

"They are friends of the Black Bear," Applebee said, as if that endorsement was all Joyce needed to make him charter an aircraft and immediately head down the North Shore.

"Is it a civil or criminal case?"

"Criminal."

"What's the charge?"

"No arraignment yet. They want you to get your client off before there is one."

"Who is 'they?'"

"I am not at liberty to say. But don't you worry about your fee. The Black Bear will guarantee it. They will put your fee in escrow if you ask them to."

"Did 'they' tell you what the criminal charge will be?"

"No."

"What do you think the charge will be?"

The voice at the other end of the line hesitated, then said, "Murder. First degree murder."

The muddy root-woven trail at Grand Portage two hundred miles east of Duluth had its own dark shadows. The portage, in swamp and on exposed granite outcropping from Lake Superior to the abandoned site of Fort Charlotte, is nine miles long and uphill all the way.

Three shadowed forms, one wearing a businessman's suit, white shirt, and tie, and two slender figured women dressed in casual attire, struggled to carry an overturned canoe across muck and mire. Its weight caused them to sink to their shoe tops and scramble for footing. The man, his suit coat open and tie twisted at the unbuttoned collar, held the craft's stern with one hand and grasped two wooden paddles in the other.

Above the treetops seagulls turned in lazy circles on invisible air currents, as if drifting on an airy carousal.

There was movement on the trail behind the struggling figures. The man turned and looked.

A guttural voice cut across the portage clearing. The intonation was clear, perfect English, with a Canadian lilt to its ending.

"Who steals the paddles belonging to Yellow Fox?"

The three set down their load.

"Will you look at that?" The man, Axel Denek, breathed his words. The women who accompanied him were slim, with long athletic legs, small breasts, and coal black hair. Their skin was flawless. Even in unkempt jeans and jackets over khaki shirts, the girls were attractive.

Standing at the edge of the woods in the light of early morning, a shotgun cradled in the crook of one arm, holding a handful of ugly metal traps, was an old man. Scraggly hair grew on his face and hung down his back. The face appeared not to have been washed. The man wore leggings, a breechcloth over khaki pants, and oversized moccasins that extended past the ankles. Across the chest the jacket was pierced by quills, which were stitched in an erratic pattern. From his belt hung two carrying bags and a knife. The most arresting thing about the ugly Indian was the twist of yellow fox fur wound around his head.

The girls stared at the man in disbelief.

Axel Denek dropped the paddles with a clatter. "We were only going to borrow them," he explained.

The black sunken eyes of the wild man stared at the two young women and then back at Axel Denek. With the shotgun, the Indian waved the three over to a log in the center of the clearing. The movement revealed that the cuffs of the jacket were also decorated with quills. As he walked sideways, keeping his gun pointed at them, the three could see that the leggings the old Indian wore partially covered the trousers. They had been cut with the hip portion higher and slanted to the crotch. The leggings were tied to the belt beneath the carrying bags.

"Who is this?" whispered Axel.

The old Indian pointed the barrel of the shotgun at the white man's throat. "Yellow Fox," he said.

Neither girl showed fear of the old man, but they obeyed his directions. The Indian motioned for them to kneel at the log. He stood on the opposite side continuing to point the shotgun.

"We weren't stealing anything," protested Axel.

The Indian, with a wave of the gun barrel, cut him short.

"Sit!" he ordered.

Both girls dropped down on the wet ground cross-legged facing the fallen tree trunk. With difficulty Axel assumed the same position. He grabbed the log to keep from falling backwards.

"Closer," motioned the Indian.

The three inched forward until their knees and crossed ankles pressed against the bottom of the log. With the barrel of the gun, the Indian tapped the trunk of the tree and said, "Put your hands there!"

Each spread their palms on the top of the log, and stared at the weaving gun barrel. Yellow Fox dropped to his knees opposite Axel Denek. He gave a warning look to the girls.

The Indian leaned the shotgun against the fallen tree with the barrel pointing at Axel's forehead. The old man shook loose one of the metal traps and set it on the log. Slowly he pried the jaws of the trap apart until they lay flat and the trigger pan that supported the bait clicked and locked the rusty metal in an open position. Still holding the trap apart, the Indian in his guttural voice spoke to Axel Denek.

"Take hold of the pan!"

An ashen color went across Axel's face when he realized what the man was telling him to do.

"Now!" instructed the old Indian in a deadly voice.

Very gingerly Axel placed his right hand between the jaws and fearfully grasped the pan in the center of the trap. The Indian withdrew his own hands and sat back on his haunches.

The eyes of the two girls and Axel were riveted on the ugly snare. Each of the jaws had triangles of sharpened teeth that interlocked when the trap was sprung, seizing its quarry with bone shattering force. Perspiration beaded on Axel's forehead as he tried to keep his hand from trembling. The man had forced Axel to let his hand become the bait on the trap, and he dared not move the trigger pan upon which his hand rested.

The old Indian looked over at the girls. They remained seated with their palms down on the log and their fingers spread wide. Axel pressed his left hand on the tree trunk as a prop to steady his body, so as not to move the hand that was the bait.

Yellow Fox stared at the three with blank animal eyes. Axel felt a burning between his legs as his bladder emptied.

CHAPTER TWO

In the Arrowhead Country of northeastern Minnesota, several thousand acres are set aside as a reservation for the Northern Ojibwa Indians, who are members of the Grand Portage band of the Chippewa. Errol Joyce first represented the tribe when many of their number marched with the Sioux in civil disobedience demonstrations on the Mandan Indian Reservation. It was in a Bismarck, North Dakota jail that the lawyer first met the iron matriarch, Marie Saulturs. In later years, the lawyer helped the famed woman chief obtain financing for construction of the tribe's hotel and convention complex at the Pigeon River border crossing and for the purchase of Wedgewood-Ben, the tribe's profitable truck line. Both the hotel and the truck line provided jobs for the Indians in northern Minnesota's depressed economy and were the source of much conflict and intra-tribal struggle.

Marie Saulturs had a Masters Degree from the School of Economics, University of Chicago. She was not only the tribe's first woman chieftain, but she was also the mother of twin daughters who were enrolled on the Cloquet campus of the Fond Du Lac Community College.

Marie and her friend, Tom Boushey, stood on the front porch of her home. The unpainted frame house was on a hillock inside the boundaries of the Thunder Bay Reservation, a box building of six rooms with black tar paper nailed on its unfinished back side and on the gables at the ends of the pitched roof. Bare slabs of wood outlined clean windows that sparkled in the first rays of sunlight. The clean swept porch, grand view of the Sawtooth Mountains and its lush forest muted the reservation's aura of poverty. The Indian woman and the man watched, in silence, the sun rise and display its panorama of colors in the groves of paper birch, aspen, and pine. A breath of morning breeze stirred the hem of Marie's pale yellow printed silk skirt and bent the brim of her hat.

"Do you ever get tired of looking at it?" she whispered. Marie rested her gloved hand on Tom's arm and lifted her chin toward the horizon.

"Never," said Tom.

"When we were on the marches on the Mandan Reservation in the Dakotas," said the woman, "it was the memory of our mountains and lakes that sustained me, and it was that way when I was attending college classes down in the city," she added.

"I never did like that open country in the Dakotas," said Boushey. "I missed the trees and the waters."

Marie had shared an important part of her life with Tom. "Remember the horrible, horrible week we spent in the jail cells in Bismarck before Errol Joyce got us bailed out?" she asked.

Tom reached out and placed his hand over the woman's. " I remember," he said. The touch of his rough hand brushed the softness of the silk of her glove and a curious feeling ran up through her arm.

"Those were the longest days of my life," breathed Marie. "We never saw the sun or the sky—nothing but artificial lights in gray rooms without windows. We were so crowded," she remembered, "I thought I would go mad."

"That was a long time ago," said Tom.

Marie Croche Saulturs was the mother of three daughters. Her youngest was still in grade school. The woman wasn't certain where Anton Saulturs, her husband, was - she guessed in Saskatchewan. She was elected the first woman chief of the Northern Ojibwa Tribe. Her people were scattered north of Lake Superior from Quebec to Winnipeg, but mostly they were settled on government lands administered by the United States Department of Interior. Theirs was the Thunder Bay Indian Reservation on the tip of the Arrowhead. Their sister tribe, the Southeastern Ojibwa, were settled in Michigan and in upper Ohio. The tribe of Plains Ojibwa were spread across the flat lands of Manitoba and Saskatchewan, west of Lake Winnipeg. The ancient people called themselves Anishinabe, but after the French and English pushed into their homeland, they became known as Ojibwa, members of the Chippewa band—hunters, fishers, and gatherers of wild rice—whose lives and work were closely tied to the seasons of the year and resources of the land.

Marie Saulturs was one of a new breed, a new generation. Like her protagonist, Engel Tormudson, she was born and educated on the reservation and went off to college to help prepare their people to cope with the encroachment of modern civilization - its destructive pollution, its roads constructed for tourists, its clear-cut logging by pulpwood contractors, and the posh resorts of owners who sought to install urban conveniences in the middle of their wilderness.

The new breed of Indian had the responsibility for preserving Ojibwa culture and traditions, while integrating the business of the tribe into the changing economy, north and south of the border, with which the tribe was forced to cope.

Since her return from college, Marie went about her tasks

dressed, some said, with desperate respectability, but she said to inspire confidence in the women who had stayed behind on the reservation. She wore double-breasted wool suits in the winter and silks in the summer. On her most casual occasions, the Indian chieftain wore a shirt-dress of cotton twill, sometimes cotton twill trousers, but she always wore gloves. Suede, wool, cotton, even silk and linen, the woman had drawers full of gloves. Marie confided to her daughters that gloves identified a lady, and she was determined that women of her reservation be viewed as ladies.

The sun rose above the horizon, and the sky was lit with a brilliant glow.

"My daughter is not dead!" said the mother finally.

Tom didn't reply.

"I know it is not Zona," whispered the mother.

"When the school called," said Tom softly, "they said that it was Zona."

"But," interrupted Marie, "they also said the girl was wearing a wedding band, and Zona never wore a wedding band!"

"They want you to go down to Duluth to look at the body," said Tom. "Are you going to do it?"

Marie nodded. "Yes," she said quietly. "But I know that it is not Zona."

"When did you last hear from your girls?" asked Tom.

"Sunday morning." The woman looked over at her childhood friend. "They usually called me every Sunday morning. They were carrying a pretty full course load during the summer term. Their laboratory classes were on Saturday so they always waited until Sunday to call me."

The sun highlighted the woman's blue-black hair. Her handsome, classic features, silken smooth, appeared much younger than thirty-seven years. Despite her age, the woman exuded a rich, fawn-like beauty that complimented her tasteful wardrobe. Her eyes were quick gray-green, watchful eyes that missed nothing. She wasn't tall, but she held herself like a queen. Tom adored her.

"Did they say anything about being gone, or leaving, or going off somewhere?" asked Tom.

"No," the mother shook her head. "Zona has done that before, maybe this time she and Nina went off together."

"Without telling you?"

Marie nodded. "They're both pretty independent," she said. "One time Zona went off with a bunch of college students to Texas. Nina has never done anything like that, but Zona might have talked her into going some place with her." Marie looked across at Tom. Shadows of apprehension reflected in her eyes. "They said the dead girl was wearing a wedding band. Zona never wore a wedding band," repeated Marie.

She spoke to the Indian in a tone that was asking for reassurance. Tom put his arm around the woman's shoulder and drew her to him as she tried to conceal her dread.

"I'll go down to Duluth with you," said Tom. His gesture contained an intimacy that comforted the Indian woman.

Marie buried her face on his shoulder.

As his flight left the runway at Devils Track Lake, the lawyer thought of the many times he had flown off the water adjacent to the airport in Jan Kiel's De Havilland Beaver. "My baby," she had called the pontoon craft the first time Joyce had ridden in it. The charter's pilot turned south and west to follow the Superior shoreline. Out of the aircraft's window, Joyce could see a dark ribbon of clouds hanging over the Quetico-Superior wilderness, where travel is still by pack and canoe over ancient trails of the Indians and voyagers. He hoped that the rain in the forecast would hold off long enough that he could fly to Cloquet and return to Grand Marais before a storm arrived. Judge Dorothy Clemens will call her court docket in Cook County tomorrow, Joyce thought. He needed to be there when she did.

The aircraft gained altitude and followed highway 61 to Duluth. The lawyer turned his attention to the Black Bear.

Errol Joyce was the only white man, and the last witness, the Indian tribes asked to testify on their behalf before a congressional committee in Washington, D.C. when it considered legislation creating the Indian Gaming Act of 1988. He remembered the effect the Indian delegation from the upper Mississippi bands had on the Senate sub-committee.

The chairman of the committee had interrupted his statement.

"Mr. Joyce, majority counsel to this committee tells me that the Chippewa bands of Minnesota had agreed that the testimony they would offer this morning would be completed by our noon recess. This afternoon the committee is scheduled to hear testimony of accountants on the economic issues of the proposed Indian gaming legislation. It is almost noon. Can you complete your statement in the next few minutes?"

Joyce nodded, "My point is that because the Government broke its treaties it created the poverty of Native Americans on the Minnesota Reservations. Congress should pass this legislation that will create a gaming industry that will help alleviate poverty." Joyce paused. "But before I stop let me tell you what our government did in Minnesota. The Government took the treaties it broke with the Lake Superior bands and consolidated them into the infamous agreement known as the Treaty of La Pointe."

"Even if we ignore the inequity of that treaty which exchanged rich land around Lake Superior for confinement on the Fond Du Lac Reservation, we cannot forget the deliberate killings of men, women, and children that followed."

"Instead of delivering promised food, blankets, and agricultural tools to the Chippewa Nation at the west end of Lake

Superior in the summer month of August, as promised, the United States Government waited and delivered them to central Minnesota at Mille Lac in October. Hundreds of Ojibwa men, women, and children froze to death when they went to get them."

There was a silence in the chamber.

After an interval the lawyer rose. "That completes my statement."

The chairman nodded. Silently the entire Indian delegation filed out of the room. That same night Joyce watched as the Indian Gaming Act was voted out of committee onto the floor of the United States Senate where it was enacted as law the following day.

At Joyce's request his pilot circled their aircraft over acres of cars and buildings before making the approach to the runway at Cloquet, Minnesota.

From the air 2,000 feet above it, the Black Bear Casino had the appearance of a strange pre-historic fish that had crawled up the St. Louis River from the depths of Lake Superior. The casino was 61,000 square feet built in the round with a strange looking saucer overturned in the middle of its roof. Extending out from it to the west was a straight-line tail like that of a stingray. The tail was a hotel of 158 rooms that was connected by a skywalk to the gambling auditorium, the Black Bear Grille, and the Bears Den Sports Bar and Lounge. Joyce knew it contained 1,000 slot machines, 24 Blackjack tables, and tables for Bingo and Video Keno. He had prepared the legal papers in which the band applied for its gaming license.

Beside the tarmac landing strip, a series of rough and rugged hummocks filled with hazel brush, rocks and muskeg, black flies, and mosquitoes created a swamp which was impassable during the summer months.

Sam Applebee was waiting at the airport when the plane landed. The two men exchanged civil greetings but did not shake hands. Applebee squeezed behind the steering wheel of a pick up truck with the Black Bear logo on its doors. Joyce sat beside him. Only one exchange took place in the cab during the short drive to the casino.

"You going to tell me who called me down here?" Joyce asked.

"You will know them when you see them," was Applebee's non-committal reply.

When Errol Joyce stepped to the door of the conference room hidden behind Sam Applebee's office, two men were waiting, standing next to the window.

Joyce could see the Canadian executive standing before him still had a familiar military bearing. From past dealings, Joyce knew he was military. Adam MacKenzie had served as Reserve Brigadier General of the Canadian occupation forces in Korea. The man with him, Omer Wallace, had been MacKenzie's roommate in college and had followed him into his father's company, Canada's famous Neville Mines, LTD. And for a short time followed as a member of MacKenzie's general staff in Korea. Wally once confided to Joyce that MacKenzie never allowed him, or the members of the Neville Mine's staff, to refer to him as General; he preferred to be called "Chairman," the same title his father was known by among family and friends.

"Good morning, Mr. Joyce," the chairman said affably. Wallace, standing by the window, only nodded.

Errol Joyce remained standing. He ignored the two men across the room and without turning his head said to the man behind him, "Applebee, I thought you said someone from Las Vegas was flying in to meet with me?"

Before Sam Applebee could answer the taller man spoke quietly, almost civilly, "We did, Mr. Joyce. We are on our way back from Nevada to Toronto and just stopped off to visit with you." The man signaled for Sam Applebee to leave and close the door. He waived his hand for Joyce to take a seat at the table.

Errol quietly said, "Mr. MacKenzie, I thought you and your friend Wallace understood what my legal opinion was. Nothing has happened to change my mind. You are not United States Nationals and you are not members of the Chippewa band. You can't hold an ownership interest in any of the Minnesota casinos because you can't qualify as owners under the Indian Gaming Act."

"Please sit down, Mr. Joyce. Wally and I didn't come here to discuss your legal opinion about the gaming law. We came here to employ you to defend a friend of Neville Mines in a criminal matter."

Joyce sat in the offered chair.

Neville Mines, LTD was a Canadian venture controlled by the MacKenzie family of Toronto, Canada. Joyce became acquainted with the company and its officers when the corporation had explored several ways it might acquire an ownership interest in successful Indian casinos. The Canadian company's last effort was the creation of a U.S. subsidiary for which Joyce refused to issue an opinion saying the subsidiary could merge with the Indian bands' gambling operation on the reservation.

"If you are not still interested in acquiring the Indian gambling operations on the reservation, why did you send word for me to meet you here at the Bear?"

"I didn't say we were not still interested in the casinos. I said I have a proposition for you. No conflict of interest," MacKenzie assured him.

There was a rapping sound.

Sam Applebee opened the door and stepped inside. "Sorry to interrupt, but they said this was important." Omer Wallace walked to the door and took a manila envelope from the man who left closing the door again. MacKenzie motioned Wallace to leave the envelope on top of the briefcase and turned back to Joyce.

"Applebee has told me what you want. You want me to work for you on some criminal case. I don't want to work for you."

"This is a rather special case to us, Mr. Joyce. We will pay your asking price for taking on the client."

"Why is Neville Mines interested in a first degree murder case?"

"Who told you there was any murder case?"

"Applebee did."

MacKenzie looked over at Wallace.

Joyce waited.

"Mr. Joyce, we know you to be a man with excellent courtroom experience. One of our colleagues has been arrested and accused by the State to be a murderer or an accomplice to a murderer. Our friend will be summoned for arraignment in Circuit Court in about two weeks. I want you to get a delay in his arraignment, for say, six weeks. That is all we need for you to get the court to dismiss the State's claim. We need you and your legal skill for six weeks, two months at the most."

"No trial? You are not looking for a lawyer to defend him?"

MacKenzie shook his head. "Won't be necessary. There will be no trial if you delay the arraignment for us."

"Who is the client?"

"A man named Gary Faulks."

"He from here?"

MacKenzie again shook his head. "No, but he once lived in St. Paul."

"Why don't you get a member of the criminal bar in the Twin Cities or in Duluth?"

"We think you are the man we need, Mr. Joyce. You know the judge and the lawyer on the other side as well as anybody. We believe you will win a delay for us."

"Where did the killing take place, where is the venue?"

"St. Louis County."

"Every lawyer in Duluth knows the prosecuting attorney in St. Louis County and also the judges that live there. Why send for me?"

"Because the arraignment is going to take place in Cook County. Your county at the request of the prosecuting attorney."

"The prosecuting attorney of St. Louis County can't get a change of venue for the arraignment."

"He can if you consent to do so for your client."

A hint of suspicion began to crawl across Joyce's mind. "When did this murder occur?"

"Last night."

"On a college campus?" Joyce asked.

MacKenzie nodded.

"Was your guy caught near the scene with a pocket full of credit cards and jewelry?"

Again MacKenzie nodded.

"The Saulturs girl?"

"That's what they say," MacKenzie replied.

Through all of their conversation, Omer Wallace sat passive with one hand on the briefcase and an envelope lying on the conference table.

"No way!" Errol Joyce said.

"You haven't heard the rest of the story," said MacKenzie softly.

"What is the rest of the story?"

"You have a friend who is going to give us problems. She is going to help the State prosecute the case, and she is going to try to get an immediate arraignment. You are the only one who knows her well enough that you can keep that from happening."

Errol Joyce remembered Jan Kiel's passionate words. "How do you know she is going to get the appointment?"

"Her boss the Attorney General down in St. Paul has already told her that she can have the appointment. I talked to him."

"Jan Kiel just learned about the killing this morning," Joyce protested. "I am the one who told her. Has she already called St. Paul?"

"She had by the time I got to talk to him. He said your lady friend wanted the assignment and he gave it to her."

"How do you know so much about what is happening in the case? The killing just occurred twenty-four hours ago."

"Neville Mines has its sources," said MacKenzie.

"Then, have your sources told you that I have a personal relationship with Jan Kiel who will prosecute the case? Have your sources told you the victim Zona Saulturs was a close personal friend of Jan as well as to me?"

"That's no problem, Mr. Joyce. Your client Mr. Faulks will waive conflict of interest claims for you and the State. I have every reason to believe you will win a postponement of the arraignment and get the charge against our friend dismissed before the arraignment is held."

Joyce shook his head. "Mr. MacKenzie, I don't like you. I don't like the way you and your company do business. There is no amount of money you can pay me to get me to take the other side of that case from Jan Kiel."

"I wouldn't say that if I were you, Mr. Joyce."

Errol Joyce leaned across the table. "Are you trying to scare me? If you are you don't know me very well, Mr. MacKenzie."

"Mr. Joyce, everyone is afraid of something."

"And you think that if Neville Mines can't buy my services that it can scare me into defending your man Faulks?"

MacKenzie thought for a moment and turned to Omer Wallace. He held out his hand. Wallace handed over the manila envelope. MacKenzie peered at the flat sheet of paper inside it and slid the envelope across the table.

"Congratulations, Mr. Joyce," he said softly. "You are going to be the father of a baby girl."

Joyce was caught off guard. "How do you know it is going to be a girl?"

MacKenzie pointed to the envelope. Joyce pulled out the contents. The stiff paper had an image printed on it.

"You can tell your child's sex by the ultrasound picture," said MacKenzie.

"You son-of-a-bitch! How did you get this?" Joyce's hand trembled as he held the image printed on the piece of paper." There was no mistaking the identity. Black block letters on the border contained the name of the patient, Jan Kiel, the date of the image, and an admittance number. Curled in an out-of-focus ball inside the mother's belly was their child. It was the first time that Joyce had gotten to see the image of his daughter.

"We know many things about your wife, Mr. Joyce."

"Jan and I have not married," the lawyer said, staring down at the paper.

"So I was told," mused MacKenzie, "but she is your daughter, is she not?"

A dark presence seemed to have settled in the lawyer's chest. "Where did you get this?" he insisted.

Adam MacKenzie hunched down on the desk. He spoke in a whisper. "We learned many things about Miss Kiel in the short time we have known about her. Her blood type. The octane of the aviation fuel her aircraft engine burns. The amount of wear on the tire treads of that old car of hers. We have learned a lot in just a couple of hours. We will learn more. Understand, Mr. Joyce, this is simply a business matter we are negotiating here. We want you to win this case for us, and you want to see that the mother of your child remains unharmed."

"You are threatening me?"

"No, no! I have made no threats. Mr. Wallace here will vouch for that. We are simply asking you to accept our offer of employment and delay Mr. Faulks' arraignment so we can be sure you get charges against Mr. Faulks dismissed."

"And if I don't?"

"Who knows?" MacKenzie shrugged. "The mother could take a fall or perhaps a mishap with the mother's plane, who knows. She does still fly despite her condition, doesn't she?"

Joyce didn't respond. He tried to read the executive's face, but his features were inscrutable.

"You are bluffing."

MacKenzie's eyes turned to flint. "Mr. Joyce the last time anyone said those words to my face was in a little village outside Pusan. He was a North Korean collaborator hiding behind his family – old people and kids – in the doorway of a concrete block building. I personally cut them all down – nine of them – with the automatic rifle one of my aides was carrying. No one has accused me of bluffing since then." The man's tone was steel hard and cold. "Isn't that right, Wally?"

Wallace nodded.

The lawyer felt trapped. Joyce feared nothing from these thugs for himself, but he knew there were hundreds of ways that others could cause Jan Kiel harm – ways, neither he nor the police could protect her from. For Jan's own safety he had to tell her. But if he did, he knew how impossible it would be to keep Jan quiet. The moment she found out she would go right to her friends in the AG's office. And if she confronted MacKenzie himself, it would only make things worse. Omer Wallace would contradict every word Joyce said; probably deny the conversation even took place. Applebee would be of no help. He wasn't in the room.

"Mothers do abort in the last month of their term, I am told." MacKenzie spoke almost in a whisper.

"You are a miserable son-of-a-bitch," muttered Joyce. "Why do you need me to defend your man Faulks?"

"Once your lady friend was assigned to the case, we knew she would do all she can to get Faulks arraigned in Cook County where the case is going to be sent by the State. Unless our man Faulks is turned loose without an arraignment there will be a trial. Maybe just a short one when they find out he did not kill the Indian girl, but just the same there will be a trial. Mind you, Mr. Joyce, Neville Mines does not want a trial of any kind. We do not want Faulks to take the witness stand for any purpose."

The executive lowered his voice again.

"We wanted you in the first place, which is why we got Applebee to arrange for you to fly down here. But it turns out you know the lawyer that has been assigned to the case, and you know her better than any other lawyer in the State. You are a good lawyer, Joyce. You should know how to handle Miss Kiel. You should be able to get the arraignment put off until we get you what you need to show Gary Faulks is not guilty."

"Your man had her credit cards in his pocket when he was caught two blocks away from the dormitory. What makes you think Faulks is not guilty of killing Zona Saulturs?"

"Mr. Joyce, your client Gary Faulks was merely holding Zona Saulturs' credit cards. Keeping them for her at the time he was arrested, which is perfectly legal. The State can never prove he killed Zona Saulturs."

"How do you know that?"

"The Indian girl is not dead."

CHAPTER THREE

Noon in Minnesota is one o'clock in the District of Columbia. Two government employees, Doctor Ivella Zahn, Assistant Regional Director of the Bureau of Indian Affairs, and Alejandro Doman, Regional Counsel of the Office of Solicitor General, sat on a park bench at the edge of the Chesapeake and Ohio Canal, just off Thirtieth Street in Georgetown.

Ivella, a big woman with a soft sag beneath her chin, tasted her spoon of yogurt, her late lunch, and listened to the instructions from the mustached and swarthy government attorney who sat on the bench beside her. Perspiring joggers with lanky frames and less energetic strollers passed behind them on the hard cinder path that ran alongside the waterway the National Park Service had restored with stone and wood.

In front of the couple, water gushed from cracks in the closed wooden watergate. Overhead a commercial jet transport maneuvered above the Potomac River as it made its final approach to Washington, D.C.'s National Airport.

"The legal point you must keep in mind throughout your testimony," explained the lawyer, "is that the Treaty of 1854 does not preempt state law and therefore does not deprive the Minnesota courts of jurisdiction over the Ojibwa dispute."

"And you lawyers think that is what the treaty says?" asked Dr. Zahn, licking her spoon. She wore her hair away from her face. She was dressed in a matronly business suit.

"That is the Solicitor's position." The lawyer was going bald and as he spoke, he pulled wisps of hair over the exposed spot.

Alejandro Doman looked around. He and the Assistant Regional Director of the Bureau of Indian Affairs had agreed to meet during the lunch hour outside of their offices so they could frankly discuss the government orders. The job of the Regional Counsel was to help prepare the Government's witness, who had been subpoenaed to testify in the dispute between members of the Ojibwa band; testimony which was scheduled to be heard by a judge in Grand Marais, Minnesota.

"And, because the Solicitor General says that, then that's what the Federal Government says - is that what you're telling me?" There was skepticism in the woman's voice.

"You must understand, Doctor, that when you are testifying out there in Minnesota tomorrow, you are testifying as a representative of the United States Government. As spokesman you must state the Government's position."

"The Solicitor General's position," corrected Dr. Zahn.

Her irony was not lost on the lawyer. "On this point," said Alejandro in his thick, clotty voice, "the Solicitor General is the government!"

The woman pointed her spoon at the lawyer. "That's only one man's opinion of what the law is," she said.

"The legal authority for the Government's position is the

concern of our office, not yours," reminded the lawyer. The words hung in the humid air between them.

Dr. Zahn rose and walked over to the trash container and tossed in her cup and spoon. The park bench was washed with sun and shadows from the overhanging trees. She wiped her hands with a napkin that she took from her purse and returned to the bench.

Carefully the woman spoke her thoughts. She knew that whatever she said would be recorded in the report the lawyer would make after she caught her air flight to Minnesota. "Alejandro," her voice was soft and reasonable, "you know the terms of the treaty as well as I. What the Solicitor is proposing that I do is to again break our government's contract with the Chippewa Nation just like it has done with every contract it has made with the Indians in the last two centuries."

The woman sat back on the bench. "I've pulled all the old files I could find on the Treaty of 1854, and it's appalling to read what we did back then to that tribe. The treaty with the Chippewas allowed mining in Wisconsin, Michigan's Upper Peninsula, and on the North Shore of Lake Superior. In an earlier treaty it was agreed that the Chippewas would get payment in food and clothing for their land, and this was to be made at La Pointe on Madelaine Island, which was an area centrally located for the Chippewas."

Her eyes flashed, but her anger was controlled.

"The Government's files show that President Zachary Taylor in 1850 ordered the payments to be made at Sandy Lake further west in Minnesota. The Chippewas protested, but they went to Sandy Lake anyway. And the United States held up the food and clothing shipments until late November. By then winter had set in, and the Chippewas were dying of starvation. Some made it back to their homes determined to keep their lands. One file shows the state legislatures, Michigan particularly, tried to get the Federal Government to let the Chippewas alone, but we made the Treaty of La Pointe anyway. That treaty took away the entire northwest section of

Minnesota with the exception of Fond Du Lac, Nett Lake, and the reservation at Grand Portage."

Dr. Zahn spoke as if she had committed the files to memory. "The Chippewas traded land for payments of money and supplies. The government signed into the treaty of 1854 an agreement to furnish fish nets, guns, ammunition, blacksmiths, and farmers to show them how to farm."

The woman paused.

"Have you ever been to the Arrowhead Country in Minnesota?" she asked.

Alejandro shook his head. "I've never been out there," he said in an empty tone.

"Anybody who knows the country around Grand Portage," said Dr. Zahn, "knows you can't even plow it, much less farm it, and Nett Lake is basically a swamp. Fond Du Lac on the St. Louis River was once excellent fishing and hunting ground, but too small to support very many people."

Overhead another whining jetliner drowned out their conversation. The woman and the lawyer waited. After the sound died, Ivella continued, "When I was reading the files and preparing for my testimony, I learned that our government made five different treaties with the Chippewas, and it broke every one of them. Congress set up a U.S. Claims Commission to investigate the Chippewas' complaints about land fraud and the broken treaties."

"The Commission reported that the Mississippi and Superior Chippewa bands legally retained title to the lands covered by the treaty. That's why I wanted to talk to you away from the office, Alejandro," explained the woman. She spoke slowly, feeling her way. "The Government's files do not support the opinion of your Solicitor General!"

The lawyer prudently said nothing. He looked around uncomfortably to see if they were being overheard.

"Do you know how much land those Indians gave up for those treaties?" Ivella asked quietly.

Alejandro shook his head. Doctor Zahn took a sheet of paper from her briefcase and read aloud, "Fifteen million acres were ceded in 1837, twelve million acres were ceded in 1842, nine hundred thousand acres were ceded in 1854, and six million acres were ceded in 1866, along with some lessor amounts that the Government picked off at various times." She put the paper back in her briefcase. Her words had bite. "The Indian Claims Commission has said that those transactions were illegal because the Government breached its contracts."

"It should not be necessary for you to discuss the merits of the treaty in your testimony," the lawyer said with a cautionary lift of his hand. "The treaty matter will be resolved on the legal question of whether or not the judge has authority to remove the chief of the Ojibwa band from office and order new tribal elections."

The lawyer knew that Dr. Zahn's position on political issues was as sensitive as his own. "'State's Rights!' Those are the magic words," said the lawyer. "If the judge accepts the Federal Government's position that it should not interfere with 'State's Rights', then there is no reason for you to express an opinion as to the merits of the treaty."

"You think I won't be asked if the Federal Government's files show the treaty should take precedent over state law?" asked Ivella.

Alejandro nodded. "That's right. Before you even give testimony there should be a ruling on the State's objection to further inquiry, and for you that should end it." He added, "The judge will probably have no choice but to make a finding that new elections must be held, and that the financing of the hotel and truck line with tribal funds was improper."

The lawyer leaned close to the woman. The hair on his head lay obediently in place. "The Federal Government's position is really a hands-off approach to this problem. As the Government representative giving the testimony, you should not volunteer any of your personal opinions regarding that treaty. Just support the Government's position."

"Whether it's legal, or whether it isn't?" asked Ivella.

"There is no specific law here that either side can point to," said the lawyer. "It's a matter of interpretation, and it is a 'State's Rights' issue. We're simply saying that the financing of these Minnesota corporations by the tribe is an issue for the judge to decide out there in Minnesota."

"And," said Ivella Zahn, "if the judge does conclude that tribal funds were spent on private corporations without proper authority, and if the Federal Government takes the position that the decision is up to the judge, then for all practical purposes, the Ojibwa Tribe will be bankrupted and dispersed."

The lawyer lifted his hand in protest. "That is for the State to decide."

Doctor Zahn shook her head. "I've spent my entire career in government service and almost all of it has been with the Bureau of Indian Affairs. I've done everything I could do to help preserve the traditions and culture of the Native Americans despite constant pressure here in Washington to break up the tribes. 'Integration into the mainstream of our society' are the buzzwords that have been used in this town for decades. We have people here that are intent on eliminating the tribal system and closing down the reservations. If the dissident group on the Thunder Bay Reservation have their way, and oust their chief, then, because of the financing documents the tribe has signed, the banks on Wall Street, who hold the debt, are going to foreclose on the hotel properties and the trucking line. The result is going to be that the tribe will go bankrupt and scatter."

Alejandro shrugged. He put his papers back in his briefcase. "It's not our concern," said the lawyer. "You're supposed to testify in support of the Government's position, and I'm supposed to make sure you understand what the Government's position is. However it comes down is not our concern."

Ivella picked up her purse and briefcase. They rose and stood at the edge of the canal.

"If I'm going to be in court in Grand Marais tomorrow morning, I must catch a cab and get out to the airport," sighed the woman. "The Government ought to admit in court that the broken contract is no longer valid and the tribe is entitled to conduct its affairs without interference from either the State or Federal Government," she added.

"You mean," said the lawyer, "let things return to the way they were in 1854?"

"Why not? Why shouldn't the Chippewa Nation be able to govern itself the way it did before the treaty was broken? Why shouldn't their tribal officers be able to invest tribe money the way our corporate officers invest corporation money today?" asked the woman. Doctor Zahn started along the canal path to the street where she could catch her cab ride.

The lawyer followed. "Call me from Minnesota if you have any problems," said Alejandro.

"I've already got problems," the woman replied grimly. "Problems with my conscience."

Alejandro Doman, a consummate bureaucrat, was a product of the Teamsters' political system in New Brunswick, New Jersey. His father obtained for him a low-level appointment in the Department of Agriculture in Washington, D.C. An appointment which permitted Alejandro to take night classes at Georgetown University and eventually to receive his degree as a Bachelor of Law. With family pride, he passed the District of Columbia bar examination, joined the Federal Bar Association, and obtained a transfer from Agriculture to the Office of the Solicitor General of the United States. Eventually Alejandro was attached to the Office of General Counsel whose duty it was to give legal advice to the Bureau of Indian Affairs in the Department of Interior. His father was proud of the fact that his son spent his days in the Department of Justice Building on Constitution Avenue, halfway between the nation's capital and the White House.

Alejandro arrived at his office every morning at eight o'clock and left each evening at four-thirty, five days a week, not counting the thirty days of annual leave given him as a part of his federal tenure. As his father instructed, the son married a fat lady five years his senior, whose government grade with the General Services Office was high enough to permit their combined salaries to purchase a four-bedroom tract home in a subdivision in suburban Fairfax, Virginia.

The Doman couple had no children, but the four-bedroom house was a bargain. Alejandro's wife told him they would buy it despite the increased tax base over other homes in the subdivision. The lawyer loved his wife mostly because she reminded him of his mother. She knew how to take care of him, to guide his career.

His first legal work was examining leases submitted by the Navajo Nation for government approval so Navajos could permit coal companies to open up surface mines on their reservation and sell lignite, which was in abundance. Over the years Alejandro became the Government's expert on coal and mineral leases on Native American lands. The lawyer explained to his friends at dinner parties that before a lease would be executed on Indian lands, his approval was required. Alejandro's wife was proud of the position of authority that he attained.

The Administrator of Indian Affairs was not his overseer. He was answerable only to the general counsel assigned to the Bureau and to the Solicitor. The Solicitor General was the federal lawyer whose staff provided advice to government agencies and represented the nation when its legal interests were involved.

Initially Alejandro's office had been in the basement of the building on Constitution Avenue, but after he developed his expertise, he was assigned to an upper floor. Eventually he officed in a dirty gray room with another lawyer on the third floor overlooking a bank of air conditioning compressors. His office was not of the grade that permitted them to have carpet. The metal desks at which he and his fellow lawyers worked were to one side, pushed together, and facing each other. The opposite wall was lined with four-drawer filing cabinets on top of which were stacked miscellaneous bundles of old files. Beside each desk was a wooden chair for visitors, and behind each desk was a wooden chair for each lawyer. A coat rack stood in the corner behind the only door in the room which led into a long hallway.

Outside Alejandro's door at the end of the hallway was the spacious office of the Solicitor General, a room with large windows that framed a view of the nation's capital dome. Alejandro knew that with each promotion he would move closer to the coveted office on the end.

Lawyers who were the closest to the end office had carpets, wooden desks, and leather swivel chairs. Some had sufficient rank to possess leather couches. Alejandro was determined to mark his time, avoid controversy, and let his earned seniority move him down the hall to the great office at the end.

Sometimes when he was alone at his own desk, he would tip back his chair and fantasize, his mind reaching down the hall and occupying the chair of the Solicitor. But Alejandro was a realist. He knew that his father only played a minor role in the New Jersey industrial city and did not have the political clout to get for Alejandro anything more than he had.

Alejandro remembered standing with Gus Doman on the Amtrak platform beside two suitcases anxiously waiting for the train that would take him to his new job. His father, a short, stocky man with gray hair and mustache, had told the others in the family to say their farewells to their brother at the dinner table. Gus informed his wife that only he would accompany their son to the train station. The father had said that there were things he had to say that were only for his son's ears.

So Alejandro said his good-byes to his momma and his sisters in the dining room of their brownstone house and had ridden in silence beside his father in the family car to the railroad station. During the trip he saw his father's lips move as Gus rehearsed what he was going to say to his son when the two said their good-byes.

Everyone except family called his father "Little Gus" because of his stature. But when Gus Doman fought for jobs for the men he represented, no one spoke of his height. Across the bargaining table he was formidable, a match for any size man.

Alejandro was aware that his father was regarded to be an honest member of the Teamsters Local, its secretary-treasurer and business agent. In New Brunswick, the employers of local trucking companies begrudgingly conceded that although a tough negotiator, Gus was not on the take and you could depend upon his word. The politicians always stopped in to visit with Gus in the Union office at election time despite Gus's demands of them that they bring more jobs to the workers of northern New Jersey.

Alejandro was a head taller than his father. He stood facing the old man on the platform as Gus began to give to him the words of advice that he had so carefully rehearsed.

"I've got a couple of things I want to tell you," said Gus.

He poked his finger into the front of Alejandro's coat.

"I want you to go to church like your mother said back there at the table when we were eating dinner."

Alejandro nodded.

"I want you to go on with your schooling. I don't want you to be like me. There ain't no place in this world now days for a man that's only got an eighth grade education. You know, I lost that election on the Teamster's Council to Phil Acocella because I only had an eighth grade education, and Phil had more schooling than me."

Gus looked up at his son, his eyes watched to see that he was listening. "Congressman Parino who got you your job says that the Government lets you go to school while you're working for it. So you go on with your schooling, understand?"

Alejandro nodded again. He watched as his father licked

his lips and prepared to speak the most difficult of the words that he had rehearsed.

"I want you to get yourself a good woman," said Gus confidentially. "And I want you to be careful when you get yourself one," he added. "Get a woman that knows how to keep house, how to cook, and can have kids. You can't have a family unless you got kids. She don't have to belong to the church at first, she can join later, but she's got to want to have kids, because you can't have a family without kids." Gus punched his son in the chest again to emphasize his point.

Alejandro nodded his understanding.

The father cleared his throat and looked around the platform to see if anyone was overhearing his words. Then he leaned his head toward his son's chest and said in a low voice, "When you're choosing, don't pass up the large women." Gus continued in a confidential tone, "Now days, all the guys talk about having skinny women, but a large woman knows how to cook, and," the father punched his son, "they are good at making babies."

Gus nodded his head sharply to confirm what he had said, stepped back, lifted his chin, and looked around the platform. He was finished. He had done his duty rather well he thought.

Alejandro didn't have to reply, for with a roar the Amtrak train to Washington, D.C. rolled into the New Jersey station.

The woman Alejandro chose knew how to cook, was of good health, and was of ample size for birthing babies. However, she said first she wanted to get their house and her man's career in order before she discarded her birth control pills and traded her job for home and kitchen. Alejandro's wife insisted that the office at the end of the hall could be his if he "played his cards right." According to his wife, who had counted, his office was only seventeen doorknobs away from the end of the hall. The young lawyer smiled at the thought.

Government offices in Washington, D.C. are cubicles that open off of block-long halls. When a visitor stands at the end of one of the wings and looks down the opening that recedes like a square gun barrel, the thing that impresses the visitor most is the doorknobs. There are no other wall hangings on the drab walls, and the gray tile floor seems to fade into the ceiling. But protruding abruptly on each side are a row of doorknobs all set at the same level and receding to the very last office that had the largest doorknob of them all.

Alejandro Doman never actually practiced law. The fact was he had not made a formal courtroom appearance in all of his career. His work with the Bureau, after he was promoted out of the land management division, was to serve as legislative liaison for the head of his section and to handle the sticky jobs presented to his section head. Jobs like the matter involving the quarrel taking place on the Thunder Bay Reservation of the Ojibwa Band.

Over the years, Alejandro had become acquainted with the woman anthropologist, Ivella Zahn. He had been at her side when she presented testimony at congressional hearings on matters involving the Indian agency. He had sat in audiences at civic gatherings and listened to the crowds' enthusiastic response to Zahn's articulate and well-reasoned statements on behalf of the tribes. He had attended her depositions when she was called upon as a witness in legal matters.

The two had developed rapport that permitted them to carry outside the government offices to the parkway by the Chesapeake and Ohio Canal in Georgetown the vexing problem presented by Engel Tormudson's subpoena requiring the appearance of an official from the Bureau of Indian Affairs to testify in the lawsuit in Grand Marais, Minnesota.

However, his relationship with Ivella was not so close as to keep Alejandro from coloring his assessment of the witness as he prepared his report of the Georgetown meeting for his superior, whose office was only five doors away from the

Solicitor's office.

While the lawyer waited for his superior to finish reading the written report, he surveyed the room and compared it to the cubicle he shared. By the carpet underfoot, he knew he was in the presence of a federal civil servant of high rank. Alejandro silently speculated on the number of lawyers ahead of him on the Solicitor General's promotion list.

"Well!" His superior laid aside the report. "It would appear that our witness may piss backwards on us during the course of her testimony."

"That was my thought," agreed Alejandro.

"Did you give Dr. Zahn a copy of the Solicitor's written opinion?"

"No. I read it to her but I kept the copy," said the lawyer.

The man behind the desk nodded. "It's just as well that you did," he said. He swiveled in his chair and looked out at the mall and its reflecting basin. Alejandro did not have a swivel chair, and the window view from his office was not so spectacular. He watched the other's back with a twinge of envy.

"Alejandro!" The man spun again to face the lawyer.

"Our section has a surplus in our travel allowance budget. We must spend it before the first of October anyhow, else we lose it from next year's budget. So I think you should take a plane out to Minnesota tonight and also attend the Ojibwa trial."

The head of his section leaned across the desk and nodding emphatically confirmed his decision. "If you're sitting out in the courtroom while Dr. Ivella Zahn is testifying, your presence might be what is needed to keep her from falling apart on cross-examination." The man jabbed the air with his finger. "And if there is a lawyer from the Solicitor General's office in the courtroom during the trial, that may make Errol Joyce pull in his horns."

"You want me to enter a formal appearance in the case for the Government?" asked the surprised, Alejandro.

"No," said the man behind the desk, "just make sure that

the Minnesota lawyer representing the tribal officers knows that our office here in Washington is watching him and that he better not try to intimidate the Government's witness, if he expects to keep his law license."

CHAPTER FOUR

The rising sun burned away the mist and cast shafts of light which highlighted a clearing beside the muddy trail and the thick, soft bed of moss laced among the trunks of fallen trees. The dampness of the undergrowth soaked through the clothing of the three figures seated upon the ground.

"Don't." The girl whispered her plea barely loud enough for Yellow Fox to hear.

The old Indian's withering look silenced her.

"Be quiet, Nina," whispered Zona. She nudged her sister with her knee.

Axel swallowed hard and held back a sour taste that welled in his throat. Despite the nausea, a rage built inside him. The Indian, he thought, was making him look like a fool in front of the two women. Axel pushed his free hand against the log with all his strength to brace his body to stop the trembling before it reached the metal pan of the trap.

Yellow Fox picked up his gun and cradled it in his arm. Speaking to Axel, he said in a matter-of-fact tone, "If you are a thief, then it is my right to kill you."

Denek had been staring at his right hand. Without moving his head, he rolled his eyes so he could look across at the other's face. The white man's mouth was dry.

"My God," he thought, "the old Indian is a madman!"

"For as long as man had memories, the Forest Sioux possessed the Lakes," recited Yellow Fox. His words were precise, his phrases stilted. "But the Cree, their brothers, the Monsoni, and the Chippewa, who were also known as Ojibwa, forced the Sioux out on the Plains to the west. The Monsoni and Cree moved to lakes further north, but the Ojibwa remained and became masters of the wilderness waters. In battles the Forest Sioux showed the Ojibwa how to ransom their captives."

A frown crossed the girls' faces. Nina, at the mention of the Sioux ransom, closed her eyes to blink back a tear. Every Ojibwa child knew the story of the savage demand their ancient enemy had made upon their Ojibwa forefathers.

"The Forest Sioux," continued the old Indian, "would sell back our people that they captured by allowing our fathers to cut off their fingers to pay for them. When the Sioux returned to their home, they could count coup just as easily by showing the severed finger as by showing a scalp."

Axel Denek's eyes widened as he heard the story. A cold numbness crept down his right arm.

"If you have stolen my paddles," said Yellow Fox, "then you are a thief, and you will die. But if you pay for the paddles then they would not be stolen," he explained.

Axel worked the tongue in his mouth and croaked, "How much do you want? We don't have much money."

Yellow Fox shook his head. "I will sell the paddles to you

for one finger!" said the old Indian drawing his knife from its sheath.

"What?" croaked Axel hoarsely. He watched in horror as the old Indian picked up a stick and slowly sliced it in half.

"Which finger will you sell me?" asked the old man.

"No!" gasped Nina's voice.

A glance from Yellow Fox again silenced her.

Axel Denek began to tremble. For a second time his bladder poured out a burning sensation between his legs.

The Indian looked over at the girls, then back at Denek. Something had come up behind his eyes. "Do you want to sell me one of their fingers?" he asked. "It makes no difference to me whose finger." The old Indian spoke as if he were bargaining fairly.

Both girls turned and looked at Axel. Neither showed fear. Axel was having to use every ounce of energy to keep his right hand from trembling and springing the steel trap.

"Which finger shall I cut off?" repeated the old man, looking down at the hands spread open before him. The knife was poised.

As she sat on the ground before the old Indian, Zona's mind flashed over the lunacy of the events that had brought her, her sister, and the man, Axel Denek, to the swamp clearing.

The two girls sat in their automobile, and Zona had listened incredulously to the radio announcement. The parked Honda appeared awkwardly top-heavy. An overturned canoe was strapped to its top. Its bow and stern extended beyond the bumpers to which the canoe was tied. At the edge of the roadway they could hear the surf roll in from the lake and strike the rocky shore.

"They said that you are dead!" Nina had whispered.

"I'm not," exclaimed her sister.

"And they're searching for me." Nina had added, "They have orders to stop our car if I try to drive across the border! Why would they say such a thing over the radio?"

"I have no idea." Zona shook her head, and a chill brushed through her. "Whose body did they find?" she whispered.

"I must tell Axel, and we mustn't let mother think you're dead." Nina ignored her question. "Zona! Go back! There is no use for you to treat me like a child. You don't have to come along," Nina protested.

"When we get to a telephone, I'll call and tell mother it's all a mistake," said Zona, "but I'm not going to let you go to Quebec with Axel Denek alone!" she whispered.

Nina shook her head. "You're just saying that because he now dates me instead of you!" Her words opened old wounds. She spoke with deep feelings and tried to keep her voice low. Nina's utterance revived animosities the two girls had agreed to bury when they went off to college together. The twin had not slept in her bed at the dormitory for three nights. Zona knew where Nina was spending her nights.

"Nina," said her sister, "all he has going for him is his looks. You can tell from talking to him that he's been in and out of a dozen colleges and still doesn't have a degree." Zona spoke intensely. "He says he's twenty-five, I'll bet he's thirty-five! He lied when he told us he was enrolled at the university and working on a Masters program."

Nina refused to listen.

"He told me all about that," whispered Nina. "He has his credits. He earned his degree at U.C.L.A., but he had an argument with the finance officer over fees. They refused to give him his diploma, but he has his degree," she insisted.

"That's bullshit!" whispered Zona. She tried to keep her voice from carrying to the woods. "You just believe anything anybody tells you. He's no good for you. Don't go with him!"

Nina pushed her suitcase to one side and leaned over to her sister. She breathed her words, "He loves me, Zona. He told me that he loves me."

Zona sat back on the seat. "That's just a line, Nina! The guy's feeding you a line. He wants something and he's trying to hook you. I only had to go out with him twice to know he's a four-flusher. If you go with him to Quebec, he'll dump you. This genetic thing he's talking about is a bunch of bullshit, he's using you!"

Zona looked across at the stolid face of her sister. "Nina, please! He's lied to us. He's no biochemist. He doesn't have money!"

"I know he doesn't have any money," said Nina, "but he has this deal he's going to close in Quebec. He's going to make a lot of money and help a lot of people." Nina gestured, "We'll only be gone a week. You keep the car. Axel and I can take the train from Thunder Bay after we slip across the border. All I want you to do is tell mother after we get across the border, so she won't worry - just like the time you took off and went down to Padre Island. I covered things for you," she said.

Nina and Zona were not identical twins. They didn't even look like twins after they graduated from high school, when they stopped dressing alike and stopped imitating each other's hairstyle.

The night the two girls gave the valedictory and salutatory addresses at their high school commencement was the last time the two dressed alike. They had kept their promise to their mother, and Marie reluctantly let them discard their twin identity that night after they received their diplomas and scholarships.

Both girls had high cheek bones, chiseled features, and quick, gray-green eyes. The two were fearless competitors, wise to the ways of the wilderness, and when in college, wise to the ways of the cocktail lounges at the edge of the college campus.

Nina was intense, organized, and wore just enough lipstick to show her mouth was perfect. When she finally got to choose her own clothing, she selected styles that covered her throat.

Zona, the most outgoing of the two, had a free spirit. She was proud of her breasts and always insisted on draping them with scoop-necked blouses. When she walked, her hair flew out in silky black tangles.

The fraction of a grade point difference that made Nina the valedictorian resulted from Zona's spring excursion and her tardy return from Padre Island on the Texas coast, where she vacationed with older college friends. Nina had declined to join her sister on her spring escapade. In their early years, and while in high school, they were sisters but not friends. Their renewed friendship was part of the truce they made when they went to college together.

During their freshman year both girls set aside their childhood rivalry and studied together. Each earned a four-point grade average, and would be entering the summer semester to begin their sophomore year tied for scholastic honors.

Their second year in college was to be the last one in which they shared classes. Zona wanted to become a lawyer like her mother's friend, Errol Joyce. Nina elected to follow the career of her mother and hoped her grades would be sufficient to enroll in the Graduate School of Economics at the University of Chicago. Zona never really worried about grades but wasn't certain whether she wanted to go to law school in Minneapolis or in Berkeley. Berkeley, California sounded like the most fun.

"That was different," Zona whispered fiercely. "I was with a bunch of college kids on Easter break. They weren't like this weirdo from California who's trying to get you to take him to Canada to sell his crazy idea about a genetic experiment."

"It's not a crazy idea," said Nina.

Zona was always amazed how very much like their mother her sister was when she started marshaling her arguments on a disputed point. If she had on their mother's silk dress, hat, and gloves, Nina would be a spitting image of the chief of the Ojibwa Tribe, she thought.

"Axel says that sports science is the exciting new frontier. Our amateur and professional athletes have begun to scratch the surface of what's possible from science. Not only at U.C.L.A., but Pennsylvania State University and other colleges have begun to make breakthroughs in sports medicine. They've done it in nutrition and in biochemistry. Axel says they've already begun to track hormone levels, amino acids, and the red-white blood cell counts so that we know the exact doses of nutrients that are necessary so athletes can excel without using dietary supplements or anabolic steroids that cause bad side effects."

"Nina," began her sister.

But her sister wouldn't let her interrupt. "Athletic champions have been found to have up to seventy percent fast-twitch fibers - the muscles responsible for speed - most of us have less than fifty percent."

Zona shook her head. "That's just a story he's telling."

"No it's not," denied her sister. "Axel has found this wonderful scientific breakthrough in genetics." The girl leaned toward Zona confidentially. "Champion athletes can be identified while they are still infants by genetic testing. At Laval University in Quebec there are geneticists who are working on the mysteries of why individuals excel in particular athletic activities, and Axel has the answer!"

Zona stared at her sister in disbelief.

Nina continued, "Axel found that if you alter the genetics, or the DNA, it is possible to improve a person's increase in their maximum oxygen intake by over one hundred percent!" The girl sat back with a smug look. "Axel has found a way to unravel the mystery of human DNA codes that increases the efficiency of the body's use of its fuel. He can change a person's genes to make superstars out of them."

"Think of that," she smiled at Zona. "Give an individual an absolute chance of winning by selective breeding!"

"That's crazy," hissed her sister.

"There's nothing new about this," said Nina. "Eastern European countries have used scientific means to advance their athletes' training. Axel says in the 1988 summer Olympics, what was then East Germany, with a population of sixteen million, walked away with one hundred two medals. The United States, which has a population of two hundred fifty five million people, only won ninety-four."

Nina was flushed with excitement. "Axel has found the secret to a new level of athletic excellence, but there are people who do not want him to use what he has found. I'm going to help him to get into Canada. I'm going to help him get credit for his scientific findings."

Zona shook her head in disbelief. "Why does he need you?" she asked fiercely. "Why doesn't he just go, and if he can find someone from Laval University who wants to buy his research, sell it to them?"

Nina whispered to her sister, "There are people who are trying to stop him from taking his formula to Laval University. He's had to hide from them. That's why he came to Duluth. That's why he hasn't enrolled in the university," confided Nina.

"Did he tell you that?" asked her sister.

"Yes."

"Why doesn't he go to the police?" asked Zona.

"I don't know," said Nina, "but he has his reasons."

Zona beat her arms on her lap in despair. "Nina, can't you see he's just feeding you a line. He just wants to use our car to get across the border, and he wants you to come up with the train ticket to take him to Quebec. He's just using you!"

Nina sat back. "Axel says you wanted to sleep with him," she accused. For an instant the animosity of their adolescent years revived.

"No," said Zona quietly, "He wanted to sleep with me but he didn't."

"That's not the way Axel tells it," accused Nina.

"Oh God!" said her sister. "You're as naive as our mother."

"And," rejoined Nina, "you're as irresponsible as our father."

Zona saw it was useless to argue with her sister. Axel Denek was good in the telling of his story, Zona knew, for he had first tried it out on her. Only then, when he told it, it was the secret to endorphins Axel claimed to have unraveled - that brain substance that raises the pain threshold of the marathon runner, that binds to opiate receptors in various nerve cells, to permit man to perform excruciating tasks, and, according to Axel, to be a super-man, unlimited by physical pain.

A man's deep voice called from the edge of the woods.

"Nina! Toilet paper! I need something for toilet paper!" the voice ordered.

Nina glanced uncomfortably at her sister and then pulled tissues from her purse. She opened the car door and stepped across the grader ditch at the edge of the road.

The twin watched her sister disappear into the woods. "Oh God!" breathed Zona.

The figure who stepped out of the woods with her sister appeared tall, straight, slim, and powerfully built. He reached across the grader ditch for Nina Saulturs' hand. She leaped to the roadway and thanked him. Traffic on the shore highway had picked up. The driver of a passing truck overtook them and blew his horn. Axel grinned. "Somebody else appreciates you, too," he said to Nina.

The man opened the car door on the passenger side and, bowing slightly from the waist, gestured toward the door with a flourish. Then to the twin who was still seated in the back seat, the man said pleasantly, "Nina has said that I may drive." A loose thatch of hair had fallen across his forehead, accenting his rakish good looks.

Nina turned in the seat to her sister. "It's all right isn't it?" she asked. Zona gave no outward sign of her feelings. The twin knew that neither Axel nor her sister, Nina, were pleased when she asserted ownership of her half of the car and insisted that she accompany it if it was going to be used by the couple to cross the Canadian border. The man had not been unpleasant. On the trip up the North Shore, Axel had several times tried to engage Zona in conversation, but the twin for the most part ignored him and looked over her sister's shoulder at tourists traveling the lake road between Duluth and Thunder Bay.

Axel shifted the gears and drove the top-heavy Honda back onto the highway. The man affectionately placed his hand on Nina's thigh and squeezed. "You're good to me," he said. Nina beamed. Turning his head, but keeping his eyes on the roadway, he spoke over his shoulder to Zona. "She ministered to me in my moment of need. When you're out in the woods with your pants down and you have no toilet paper, that's a moment of need!" He laughed a deep honest laugh, good-natured and sincere.

Zona stared at the back of the man's head. "How stupid," she thought.

For several miles the three rode in silence. Axel looked up into the rear view mirror into Zona's eyes. She turned away. "You were wrong about my college degree," he had said with a wry smile.

Zona gave him a quick denying glance.

"I couldn't help but overhear you two ladies talking," he continued.

Neither girl replied.

"At U.C.L.A. my major area of study was the famous 'Gavia immer'. It is the reason I chose the lake country when I decided to leave California." Nina stared out the windshield and said nothing. She had heard the man's story before. The retelling she knew was for the benefit of her sister, Zona.

"What does the Common Loon have to do with biochemistry?" asked Zona.

"I never told you I was a biochemist." The driver spoke quietly. "You just assumed I was a biochemist when I told you about my undergraduate work with marathon runners and the endorphin phenomena."

"What of the story you told Nina about discovering a genetic breakthrough in sports medicine?"

"My major at U.C.L.A. was biology," explained Axel. "You can't be a graduate biologist without studying chemistry. It was when I was doing biology lab work that I found a way to alter an athlete's DNA." He glanced at Zona again.

"But that wasn't your research project." Zona doubted the man.

"No," admitted Axel, "the title of my university research grant was 'The Common Loon of North America'. Without the grant I couldn't have afforded U.C.L.A."

"Tell us about our loon," challenged Zona.

Axel Denek grinned back at her in the rearview mirror. "Is this going to be a test?" he asked.

"Just tell us what you could possibly learn in California about Minnesota's loon."

"Well," began the driver, "what do you want to know?"

"Anything you want to tell us about the waterfowl," said Zona.

"No! No! That was clever!" Axel lifted a finger from the steering wheel. "No trick questions!" He laughed. " Waterfowl are a separate category of water birds that include only ducks, geese, and swan. The Common Loon is not a true waterfowl. You can't trick me with that one. Every freshman biology student knows the difference. Loons represent an entire order in nature, the 'Gaviformes' - they have no close relatives."

"Did you know that?" Nina turned to the back seat and asked her sister. Zona ignored the question. "What is the Ojibwa name for the loon?" Zona continued.

"Mang," replied the man. "That's also the name of one of the Ojibwa clans of the western Great Lakes. The word translates as 'loon' but also indicates 'brave' or 'proud.' I learned in my research that 'Mang' legends say loons are special messengers of the gods endowed with magical powers."

Nina laughed. "Zona, he does know our Common Loon," she said remembering the old tale retold on the reservation.

"Honest, Zona," said the driver again glancing back in the

mirror, "I was going to do my Master's thesis on the Common Loon."

"Do you know what the Ojibwa mud story is?" asked Zona.

"I know one version. According to the Ojibwa legend, during the early time when all was water, the Great Spirit asked if a creature would dive to the bottom and bring back mud so there could be land for animals to walk upon. The otter, the beaver, and the muskrat dove, but each failed. The Great Spirit appealed to the loon who dove deeply and returned with mud on his feet. The effort earned him the title, 'Loon Who Made the World.'"

"That's right!" Nina smiled back at her sister. "There aren't many outside the Ojibwa Tribe who know that story!"

"What got you interested in the loon out in California?" asked Zona. "Their migration route is down the East Coast to the Gulf."

"We have Common Loons in California," said Axel. "The 'Gavis immer' also migrates on the West Coast. It comes down from Alaska."

"Why did you choose to study the loon?" she asked again.

Axel Denek grinned sheepishly. "Because of their sounds," he said. "I think it's because my chief interest has been the loon's remarkable ability to vocalize. They communicate primarily at night when the winds are gentle and sound carries far, with four basic sounds: hoots, wails, tremolos, and yodels."

"See, Axel does know his loons," Nina said again.

Zona reminded her sister, "Studying loons has nothing to do with genetics."

Axel Denek's face lost its smile. "If you don't believe that I've made some special discoveries in genetics," he said soberly, "then that's your problem, not ours. Nina and I are going back east to Laval University no matter what you think and no matter how many guards they have at the border."

"Did you tell Nina that you're married?" Zona asked maliciously.

"Zona!" Her sister turned to the back seat. Her temper flashed.

"Well, did he tell you?" Zona asked. The girls' eyes traded malevolence.

"Your sister knows about my wife," said Axel quietly.

"Did you tell her? Or did she find out about your marriage by accident the way I did?" asked Zona.

Axel Denek compressed his lips and did not reply. Nina turned in her seat and stared ahead through the windshield.

Again the three rode in silence until the driver began slowing the car and peering into intersecting roads that led down to the lakeshore. "I've got to make a stop," said Axel finally.

"Again?" asked Nina.

"I want to do something with the canoe." Axel gave no further explanation. The driver pulled off the highway and down a rutted lane.

Zona watched the overturned metal craft bounce on the rope that lashed it to the Honda's front bumper. When the two girls had returned to the car after their rest stop in Grand Marais, they found Axel had obtained a canoe. Axel's only explanation when he tied the canoe to the top of their car was that it would come in handy to cross the border by water on one of the lakes in the event they had difficulty getting through customs at the highway border crossing.

"What difficulty?" Zona had asked.

Her sister was also puzzled but she hadn't questioned the man.

Axel put off the two with an explanation that they were going into Canada without work permits despite their intent to negotiate the sale of his scientific discovery. Axel had explained that should they be turned back at the border for that reason, he intended that they play the roles of tourists and enter Canada by one of the water routes. The canoe was necessary he had said.

Zona leaned to the driver's seat. "What," she asked frostily, "are you going to do to the canoe?"

"Work on the buoyancy chamber before we use it to get across the border," he answered without evasion. The man referred to the metal compartments at each end of the canoe that were stuffed with the same air-filled foam as life preservers. They were the canoe's flotation device.

"What's wrong with the buoyancy chambers?" asked Zona. The man didn't answer. Instead he brought the car to a halt in an Aspen grove above a shelf of rock where surf pounded against the shoreline.

"This will do nicely," said Axel.

The two girls had sat, not talking, on rocks of the Canadian shield, foundation rocks which were among the first formed after the crust of the earth cooled and wrinkled like the scum on a pot of warm soup. Quaking Aspen shivered overhead when a slight breeze touched their spade-shaped leaves. The two women gazed across the empty, flat water that extended to the horizon. Like so many silent hours they had spent together as children, thought Zona. She had hoped the truce they made when they went to college would change that for she cared about sister and she knew her sister cared about her.

For three-quarters of an hour they listened to metal sounds made by the man who had accompanied them but neither girl spoke.

When the Honda pulled back on the highway and the three resumed their journey, Zona could see bright scrape markings on one of the buoyancy chambers. The chamber in the front of the canoe had been pried open, then replaced. Zona wondered what Axel had concealed in it.

Axel tossed from the speeding car a wad of foam and a small cardboard cylinder that Zona had never seen before. The man grinned. "I don't think that will upset the ecology of our environment," he said.

CHAPTER FIVE

Eight months earlier, in the bay across from Marie Saulturs' cabin, the shadows were long in a slanted battern against the bed of reeds. The sun was dropping toward the hilltops when Marie and her two daughters set out to catch their supper.

Zona feathered her paddle back and forth in the water and made no sound as she worked the canoe in closer to the reeds, then let her hands rest, motionless. In the bow, her sister sat with her paddle laying across her knees and watched their mother cast the lure. Marie brought the rod over her head and flipped it sharply. The lure arched away over the mat of lily pads, almost to the shore, taking with it the light filament line. Slowly the Indian mother turned the crank on the reel, tightened the line, and with occasional flips of the tip of the rod, worked the lure through the reed bed.

"Let's have fishcakes tonight," their mother had exclaimed and insisted that her daughters paddle her across the bay where the reeds sprout and the northern pike did their evening feeding. Marie's fishcakes were a well-known table delight in the Boundary Waters. Most fishermen preferred the walleye or trout which had fewer bones. But the Indian mother used an old Ojibwa recipe, which called for grinding the pike, mixing it with herbs, and deep frying the patties to crispness. The result was an exceptional delight. Fishcakes, insisted Marie, had to be made with fresh caught pike to be good.

Marie gently cranked her line with gloved hands and brought the lure to the edge of their craft, then cast for the reed bed again.

The canoe drifted at the edge of the lilies. The three were in the backwater of the lake away from wind and current. Except for an occasional feathering of the paddle by Zona, the women sat in the evening solitude, each with her own thoughts.

Marie cast her line again and said with a mother's bluntness, "You girls are going to be leaving home next month when you go off to college. I think the three of us need to talk."

Zona lifted her paddle out of the water and laid it across the thwart of the canoe.

The craft drifted as their mother gave up any pretense of fishing.

"You are no longer children." She paused and dipped the lure at the end of her rod in the water and seemed to be gathering her thoughts. "I remember," sighed the mother, "when one day I was a child and then I was not." She looked back at Zona. "I had no one then to tell me, 'You are no longer a child.' I had started to menstruate. I grew breasts. Tufts of hair appeared under my arms and between my legs. I grew taller. I found it hard to manage so many changes, so much all at once. While I grew up I lived silently without anyone to tell what I felt for I had no real sister I could talk to, only cousins."

Marie turned back to the lure. She bobbed it absently in the water. "I wasn't fortunate enough to have a twin to share my feelings. I was living silently in my own personal hell without anyone to tell what I felt, without even knowing that the feelings of love and hate I had were possible to have."

The Indian mother shrugged. "Then one day I was not living like that at all. I had begun to see the past is a line; you can draw it yourself, or sometimes it gets drawn for you. Either way, there it is; your past, a collection of people and values you used to be and things you used to do; rules that you followed without question, traditions and taboos that you never dared break. I realized that our past is the person we no longer are, the situations we are no longer in."

"Before I was seventeen and went off to the Dakotas, I lived in a lodge with 'atiquon' and 'eadse' that I was permitted to love, but dared not touch. I used to sit on a lake shore with them to fish and hunt for the blueberries and wild rice. I used to sit where the sun streamed through the trees trying to explain to myself how I got to feel the way I felt. I saw the perfect world of my childhood that I had known vanish without warning. I saw sadness replace it. I used to lie naked in the moonlight with a boy I had no right to be with."

Marie stared across the water. Her daughters weren't certain whether their mother's softly spoken words were being spoken to them or only to herself. "I used to be that person, and I used to be in those situations. That was how I spent the years before I went to the protests in the Dakotas, before I went to school in Chicago."

"When Anton left," the name their mother rarely spoke startled Nina and Zona, "I told myself that I never wanted to see him again. These were words said in the way of a child; for a child might want someone dead, might even wish to do the deed herself, but would want the dead person to get up and carry on as before, only without the thing that made the child wish for the death in the first place. I had wished never to see Anton again, and my wish had become true." Nina looked at Zona. Their eyes met but neither dared to interrupt their mother.

"I felt guilty then. Guilty - I had always thought that was a judgment passed on you by others but I had learned it could be a judgment you could pass on yourself. I wished that I could have told Anton that I was sorry for everything that had happened to him because of me. I could not say that I loved him. I could not say that. Too much had happened. But Anton was good to me when I needed his animal strength to survive in Chicago."

Marie drew back her arm, and with all her strength cast the lure out into open water where the fish seldom ventured during their feeding time. The girls watched as she wiped the corners of her eyes with the back of her gloved hand. "When Anton first left, the days went by too slowly and too quickly. I could not put this period of my life behind me, and each moment felt like a ball of lead. At the same time I wanted to understand everything that was happening to me, and each day felt like a minute."

"I remember the weather especially after Anton left. The skies were hard and gray, it rained, and the rain felt like small hard nails. The sun shone sometimes but weakly as if it held a grudge. I noticed how hard and cold and shut up tight the ground was. I noticed this because I used to wish it would just open up and take me in, I felt so bad. If I dropped dead from despair as I was crossing the highway, I would just have to lie there in the cold. The ground would refuse me."

Marie placed her fishing rod in the bottom of the canoe and let its line drift in the water. She looked from Nina to Zona and said fiercely, "I wanted a sister then. I wanted- I needed my own family friend. I would look at you two girls and envy you, that all your lives you would have each other to share the same restlessness, the same dissatisfactions with your surroundings, your lives. It wouldn't have mattered to me if my sister, my family friend, had shortcomings and differences. I wanted the yoke of another's companionship. I wanted someone who would help me find the answers, tell me what to do."

There were tears in the woman's eyes. "I could not ask God what to do since the answer, I was sure, would not suit me."

"I had to make my choices without a sister of my own to help me. After I crossed that line out of childhood, I could do what suited me, as long as I could pay for it. 'As long as I could pay for it.' That phrase became the tail that wagged my dog. If I had died then when I was seventeen, it could have been my epitaph."

The Indian mother who had spoken her mixture of words and thoughts, almost in a trance, addressed her daughters intensely. "You two have argued and fought long enough. You're no longer children; long ago you crossed that line." Marie shifted sideways so that she could look at both of them. Nina had swung her feet around and sat facing her mother. "I have never understood," said Marie, "why sisters, particularly twin sisters, fought so much."

Zona compressed her lips and looked across at Nina but said nothing.

Marie continued, "I know it has not been easy for you, with Anton gone, to grow up with only a mother to raise you, and sometimes," she shrugged, "I have probably been too busy, or gone too much, to be the mother I should have been. But you are both young women now. I didn't realize how much you two detested being treated alike, wearing the same clothes, and everything I asked you to do." She sighed, "I even gave both of you the same graduation present."

Nina and Zona looked at each other. Their mother had given them identical sweaters the afternoon of their graduation, an hour after the twins had made an agreement that following the ceremonies they would tell their mother that they did not intend to dress and act like twins any longer.

Their mother continued, "But we are family. This arguing that has gone on ever since you were kids should stop." Marie looked from one girl to the other. "It is going to cost a good deal of money for you two girls to go to college. I am very proud of the grades that you got and the scholarships that you won, but Nina," Marie turned to the daughter in the bow of the canoe, "if you live off the campus like you say you want to do instead of in the dormitory with Zona, there will be more expense. But it's not just the money I'm thinking about. I don't believe that you two girls ought to leave home and live the rest of your lives like strangers. As you get older you're going to find that good family friends are just as important as friends we make from the strangers we meet. I want you two to be good family friends."

Marie Saulturs spoke quietly, "I don't know what it is that has made you two so different and so disagreeable with one another over these years, but I want you to end it before you leave our home and go to college. I want you to make a truce. Nina," she said, "I don't want you to live off campus. I think you two girls should live together and get to know each other. In all these years of growing up in our home, you two have never gotten to know each other. I want you to live as roommates for the first year, at least the first year. I want a part of your education to be to learn to like each other, truly be sisters. You don't have to be twins. You don't have to want the same things, but this next year in college will be your last chance to be family friends."

During all of their mother's monologue, neither daughter spoke.

Zona tried to make eye contact with her sister, but Nina, after her mother started talking about their differences, had turned to gaze across the open waters of the lake.

The three drifted in the canoe in silence. Marie picked up the fishing rod and idly wound the reel until the lure again dangled from the tip. She made a half-hearted cast and waited for her daughters to speak.

Finally Zona addressed Nina. "I'll share the dormitory room with you if you will."

Nina licked her lips. Her face was tight as she turned and looked directly at her sister. A mist seemed to cloud her eyes.

Their mother had seen that face before when the girls were together, almost like a woods animal, afraid to approach, that wanted to be friends.

Nina nodded. "If that is what you want us to do, Mother, then that is what I'll do," she said.

Marie shook her head. "I don't want you to do it because I asked you to do it. I've tried ever since you were little to get you two to do things that would bring you together, rather than push you apart. I want you to spend your first year in college living together because you want to do it, because you want to learn to know each other."

Nina nodded. "I'll do it if Zona will."

Zona Saulturs grinned. "I already told you that I would, Nina."

"We'll do it," said Nina.

Marie smiled. She laid her rod in the bottom of the boat and reached out and grasped each of her girls by the hand. "I love you two," she said.

Zona smiled back. "We love you too, Mother," she replied.

Nina didn't speak. She just squeezed her mother's glove tightly.

Zona was shaken from her reverie by the sound of the voice of Yellow Fox.

The portage clearing had lightened enough to show the two girls that the old Indian's face was impassive. He looked down at the trembling figure on the opposite side of the log.

"Which finger shall I cut off?" he repeated.

"Not mine," croaked Axel.

Nina looked at Axel in disbelief. Yellow Fox glanced at her and then back at the white man.

"Shall I cut off one of their fingers?" he asked, pointing the knife at the girls.

Axel could hardly get the words out of his mouth. "Not mine!" was all he would say.

The old Indian very carefully positioned the knife where the white man could see it. A silver sunburst of delicate design was worked into its leather handle. The blade glittered in the morning sun and pointed at the little finger on Nina Saulturs' right hand.

"That one?" he asked.

Axel would not answer.

Yellow Fox leaned his gun against the fallen tree. Reaching over he very carefully took hold of each of the steel jaws. Holding them in place he said, "Lift your hand."

Axel jerked his right hand off the trigger pan. Yellow Fox let go of the jaws, and they snapped shut barely missing Axel's sleeve.

"Go," ordered the Indian.

Axel bolted for the edge of the clearing.

"Take your paddles," called the Indian, "you have bought them!"

Axel looked back desperately. Then, scooping up the wooden paddles, he dashed out of the clearing. The canoe lay beside the trail.

The old Indian rose to his feet. For a long moment he gazed sadly down at the two girls. He picked up his gun and reached over and retrieved his trap and his knife.

Both girls lifted their chins but said nothing.

Yellow Fox put his knife in its sheath. He quietly gave a command. "Go home to your mother!" he ordered. With that he spun on his heels and disappeared into the woods.

CHAPTER SIX

Fifty miles north of Grand Marais on Mountain Lake, high up on the Sawtooth Range, where the Province of Ontario meets the northern border of the State of Minnesota, a tall, thin, almost cadaverous Indian slowly pushed his aluminum canoe toward the rising sun and searched for a lob pine. He had been told that the tree had a single top knot of branches, shaped by an unknown traveler who had climbed it and lobbed off its branches below the crown, so as to mark the ancient portage between Mountain and Rose Lakes.

Engel Tormudson believed himself to be wholly Ojibwa, a member of the Chippewa Nation, despite his taint of white blood. He was the brilliant grandson of a brilliant Norwegian merchant. He had been born, reared, and educated, until he went to college, on the Thunder Bay Reservation at the Pigeon River border crossing.

The Indian knew he had to cross Rose Lake and reach the Laurentian Divide before noon. Otherwise, he would miss his rendezvous with the Solicitor who had consented to advise with him.

Low on the horizon the Indian spotted the landmark. The lone tree stood out from all the others. It had a topknot as described by the elder back on the Ojibwa Reservation. Tormudson thrust his paddle with powerful strokes and made for the portage he knew would be on the shoreline below the primitive monument. The waters of Mountain Lake were smooth and flat.

South of the Laurentian Divide, the water flows east to Pigeon River where it empties into Lake Superior at Grand Portage. North of the Divide, the waters flow into Hudson Bay four hundred miles above Lake Superior.

The only way Tormudson could travel the intricate tangle of paths, lakes, and rivers was by canoe and on foot.

The Solicitor, Peter Hauck, practiced law in Duluth. He was senior partner of the law firm of Hauck and Figg. The lawyer had consented to interrupt his vacation at a campsite between North and South Lakes long enough to counsel with Engel Tormudson. The Indian had set about to gain political and economic control of the Ojibwa band, its hotel and convention center, and Wedgewood-Ben, the tribe's successful trucking line. The solicitor he had chosen had concluded Tormudson's intentions were honorable and, for a fee, consented to help his take-over bid.

At the swamp portage, Tormudson stepped onto a flat rock. He removed a Duluth pack from the bow and lifted the canoe onto the shore. He shrugged into the shoulder straps of the pack, then overturned his aluminum craft so its yoke rested on his shoulders. Blowing irritably at the swarm of mosquitoes that gathered about his face, he set off on the spongy path for Rose Lake and the meeting with his lawyer.

CHAPTER SEVEN

Ivella Zahn sat in her narrow seat and stared out the airplane window. At thirty thousand feet there was nothing for her to see except banks of clouds beneath the airliner hurtling toward Minneapolis and Duluth. She thought back to the times she had been spokesperson for the Bureau before congressional committees, courts, and at civic gatherings. She knew others regarded her to be an articulate champion for Native Americans.

"They will ask," she thought, "What is your name? And I will reply, 'I am Ivella Dorene Zahn.' And they will ask, 'Where were you born?' And, like the other times, I will reply with the truth, but not the whole truth. I will say, 'I was born in the Bronx, New York.' I will not say 'I am the bastard child of a trust fund and of a mother who was seduced by her wealthy employer, left with a bitter heart and sufficient income to rear her bastard child in middle class comfort, and to permit her child to be an anthropologist and obtain from a city college a scholarly, lonely Ph.D.'"

"They will ask me why I spent all those years in college reading all those books and wandering through all of those museums studying native North American tribes. I will tell them the truth, but not all of the truth. I won't tell them that I found among the North American Indians tribesmen who hung onto the remnants of their culture and traditions in solitary loneliness, similar to the loneliness felt by a child mothered by a recluse."

Ivella Zahn shifted in the narrow seat wedging her large frame into a more comfortable position. The clouds began to thin so she could see the ground roll in slow motion. She lay her head against the aircraft's window and closed her eyes.

She thought, "They will ask, 'Why did you choose an obscure post with the Bureau of Indian Affairs in Washington, D.C. for your life-long career?' And I will say, 'I have always had a keen interest in the American Indian.' I won't tell them that the tribes share with me the embarrassment of being bastards, of being cut off from their heritage, ashamed of receiving food, clothing, shelter, and money to exist, without love, without compassion, without nurturing."

Tears seeped out of the woman's closed eyelids and ran down her cheeks.

She would not tell them that the tribes and the Bureau were her family, the only family she ever had.

Ivella remembered the cold winter day she took a subway train under the river and climbed a slick metal stairway that opened onto the dirty, snow-lined streets of lower Manhattan Island. The tall buildings, which thrust against the skyline that the thirteen-year-old could see from her borough across the river, were overpowering, intimidating when she stepped out of the subway station and walked among them. The temperature was only a little above zero, and the snow crunched beneath Ivella's feet like metal foil. Grimy, gritty ice crystals broke with each step exposing white snow not contaminated by the filth of the city. Ivella walked close to the buildings where the snow drifted undisturbed and avoided the dirty path thronged with hurrying men and women upon errands of special importance. Ivella observed there were no other children about.

The windowpanes in the shops and offices along narrow Wall Street were covered with botanical frost shapes. The snow swept up in heaps, the ice-gritty streets, block after block, were bound together by the iron of the sky. Ivella stepped as carefully as she could to keep the dirty crust out of her shoe tops. The girl counted the numbers over the doors until she found the office building where her father worked. The same numbers that appeared upon the envelopes that her mother tore open and threw in the trash after extracting checks that paid for their food, their home, their clothing, and Ivella's schooling. Envelopes that always arrived promptly on the second day of each month.

The doorman who stood inside the lobby door out of the winter wind had laughed when Ivella asked for her father by the name she had found on the envelope's return address. The amused black man pointed her to a lady sitting at a desk in the lobby and looked on with a grin as the lady patiently explained to the thirteen-year-old that "Germania Bancorp Trust" was not the name of a man, but of a banking institution, and that Ivella was standing in the lobby of the Germania Bancorp Trust Company building.

Ivella Zahn had wiped cold tears from her eyes on the trip in the subway train as it carried her under the river and back to her home in the Bronx.

Her mother was enraged when she learned of Ivella's trip and screamed incoherently at the girl.

"He never wanted you!" The woman was livid, seething.

Her mother had put her face inches from Ivella's, and the thirteen-year-old stood trembling as the woman berated her uncontrollably. "He never wanted you," she mocked with destain, "you made a fool of yourself."

Involuntarily Ivella drew back her hand and slapped the face thrust in front of her. "Liar! Liar!" she screamed.

The woman's twisted face appeared to turn to stone. She hissed, "And I never wanted you either. I only thought your father would marry me!" With that the woman uttered the last words that Ivella ever heard her mother speak.

During the next twenty-five years in their home, and after her mother had fallen and broken her hip, in the apartment building that was converted into a nursing home, and finally in the hospital on her death bed, Ivella's mother never spoke another word in Ivella's presence. For over twenty-five years the two communicated with the exchange of notes, pencil to paper, the bare necessities of communication. At first, Ivella knew that her mother could talk, but stubbornly wouldn't. Later, after the old woman was confined to her bed in the hospital, Ivella thought her mother had not spoken for so many years that the woman had forgotten how to frame her words. At the last Ivella had sat beside the hospital bed and stroked her mother's frail arm and begged her to talk to her, to say her name, to give to her some sign that Ivella was a daughter that she wanted. But only the sounds of breathing, dry and hard, and obstructed, issued from her mother's lips.

Ivella, alone, was in the room with her mother when she died. "I didn't want you either!" were the words burned into Ivella's heart, words she could not forget, the last she heard her mother speak.

Ivella Zahn always thought of herself as being a pragmatic woman. She tried to view her mother's life and death from an authentic perspective. The woman had hated her lover with the same passion she had loved him with. She had purposefully allowed her pregnancy and the birth of a baby daughter in the hope that she would hold the man for whom she worked and to whom she had given her love. He had said he had no excuse to leave his cold marriage bed. Ivella knew that her mother had tried to give her lover that excuse, but he refused her gift. Instead he had settled upon Ivella's mother a trust fund and forced her out of his life. Ivella understood the feelings of her mother, the recluse who would not speak, but that had not made the pain any less searing. Her mother had spoken a burning truth. Her father had not wanted his baby, and her mother had not wanted her either.

The airplane stewardess paused at her row to ask if the passenger cared for a magazine. Ivella didn't answer. She kept her face turned to the window. The airplane carried her above the cloud bank west toward Minnesota, the land of the Chippewa, hunters, fishers, and gatherers of wild rice.

CHAPTER EIGHT

Errol Joyce's companion in the remodeled warehouse was P.M. Gregory, a former judge of the District Court of Cook County, Minnesota. A little man, weighing barely one hundred ten pounds, always wore undertaker black suits, black string ties, and white starched collar shirts that were too big for his long thin neck. The man's entire law career had been spent on the North Shore of Lake Superior. Other lawyers said that in his prime he was a brilliant advocate and jurist. Despite his eighty years, Joyce knew that P.M.'s hearing was sharp, his mind was still keen, and his body was as agile as someone half his age. The old judge's only infirmity was his poor eyesight. Since his retirement from the bench, P.M. Gregory stayed busy examining abstracts and land titles. When he read, the old man supplemented his thick lenses with a magnifying glass the size of a saucer.

"That Jan Kiel can be stubborn," P.M. said. "Why did she refuse to ride down with us to Duluth? Was it my car, or was it you?"

P.M.'s car was a 1948 Buick Roadmaster four-door sedan. It was one of the first built following the end of World War II. It appeared worn out, and the exterior was repainted a flat yellow color. P.M. acquired it for his fishing car. The back seat was missing. The firewall behind the back seat was also gone giving access from the front seat clear into the trunk. When the trunk was open, an eighteen-foot aluminum canoe fit but overhung the back bumper. It ran well and after a time became P.M. Gregory's only transportation on the North Shore highway and the gravel trails back to the Border lakes. But it was a big car, and Jan Kiel could have been accommodated on the front bench seat between the two men for the trip. However, she declined the offered ride to Duluth despite the fact that after her declared intention of talking to the Prosecuting Attorney of St. Louis County and University Alumni luncheon she would return to Grand Marais.

"No, P.M.," Joyce grunted. "It's not your car. It's me!"

"What the hell happened to you two anyway?" asked the old Judge. "After Jan had her fall on the slope down in Minneapolis last winter, you announced the wedding was off. One week you tell me Jan is going to have your baby, and the two of you are going to get married; the next week you tell me it is all off. What happened?"

"She never told you?"

"Errol! Neither you nor she has told anybody anything. All we know is that you two were going to have a baby and you were going to get married; Jan goes to the hospital, and then out of the blue, wedding plans are off."

"Didn't she tell you why she was in the University Hospital last winter?"

"Nope."

"...or about the accident on the ski slope?"

"Nope."

Errol Joyce looked out along the harbor and watched the waves pound as they were pushed from behind by the winds. The smell of rain was in the air.

"You going to tell me what happened?"

Joyce nodded and sat in a chair.

"During the holidays we learned that Jan was going to have a baby. We took a few days off and went down to Minneapolis to sort of celebrate and get our wits together after her doctor gave her the news. Jan didn't have any family. My folks are dead. So we went to see if we could use the university's chapel for a small wedding. South of the city along the interstate, there is a ski lodge where the university ski team competes. For our holiday we decided to spend a couple nights at the lodge and watch the annual ski jumping competition. The ski jumps were over seventy-five feet high. Jan was ahead of me, standing against the rope that was used to keep spectators back. She was off to the side where she was supposed to be when one of the jumpers came off the end of the track at an angle toward her with legs and arms windmilling. The jumper was completely out of control, probably moving forty miles per hour when he hit Jan and sent her rolling head over heels down the slope."

"Damn!" P.M. breathed the word.

"By the time we got to them, the college kid was screaming with a broken leg, and Jan was unconscious. When the ambulance guys got there, they thought Jan's back was broken. I remember it took them the longest time to strap her down and load her. During all that time she didn't say a word. It was eerie! Her eyes were open real wide and the muscles on her face were rigid. That took part of the time because the ambulance crew wouldn't move her until they got her eyes closed and bound wet cloths around her head to hold her eyelids shut. They said she was in a coma."

"Damn Errol!" P.M. said. "I didn't know that."

"Few do. She wasn't out very long. She insisted on leaving the hospital the next day."

"Why would she get mad at you over that? You didn't cause the guy to fall on her and knock her out."

"In the hospital emergency room, while they were getting her clothes off of her, they were asking me stuff like - name, address, next of kin, and the sort of things hospital nurses ask about in that kind of situation. I kept telling the doctor who was working on her to be careful because she was going to have a baby. He asked me about her pregnancy and how far along she was. He tried to talk to her, but she didn't respond. They kept damp cloths on her face. Her eyes just stayed open like her face was paralyzed. One nurse kept putting eye drops in her eyes to keep them moist."

"All the time was she unconscious?"

"Yes. When they found out she had no family, I told them I would sign the hospital papers they needed, that we were going to be married anyway. The doctor then asked me if had the right to authorize her operation."

"I asked what operation."

"He said that they were going to do a series of tests and x-rays, but he was reasonably certain that Jan had a pooling of blood on the brain that was causing partial paralysis, and blood had to be drawn off the brain at once. He and another doctor told me that if the blood started to absorb inside the skull, it would leave scar tissue which would cause additional brain damage and complications."

"What about the baby?" P.M. asked.

"That was the worst part. They said they had to have consent to abort the baby because if there was a spontaneous abortion during the brain operation, both Jan and the baby could die."

"Jesus Errol! What did you tell them?"

"What could I tell them? I was the father. I had as much right as anyone to consent to the procedure. They were looking to me for the answer. They weren't going to make the decision for me. Jan was unconscious there in the emergency room. There was no way the baby would live if Jan died. She wasn't far enough along. If they aborted the child and then did the operation to remove blood from inside her skull, there was a chance that Jan would live. I had no choice. At least I didn't think I did. I signed the papers that consented to both the abortion and the brain surgery. Shit! That was within two hours after the accident. I thought I had no choice."

"You said she wasn't out very long."

"She regained consciousness while they were rolling her cart down the hall to the operating room, before they even did anything."

"And she was alright?"

Errol Joyce nodded. "Just a headache. She refused to stay in the hospital more than one night."

"And that is what caused you two to split?"

The lawyer nodded.

"That don't sound reasonable."

"Two doctors tried to get her to stay in the hospital longer, but she wouldn't do it. One of the doctors told her that she had come near losing her baby, that what had happened to her was very significant, and they couldn't be responsible for her and her unborn child if she insisted on leaving. She asked why they thought she had come near losing her baby. They told her what the plans were for the operation. She asked them who consented to her having an abortion. They said 'the father did.'"

Errol paused.

P.M. Gregory nodded his head. "I understand now. It was that bad was it?"

Errol shook his head. "I never saw her like that before. She let out a shriek and lunged at me. Her fingernails were like claws digging into my face. It took both doctors to restrain her. They tried to explain how things appeared; that she was unconscious and how she looked to all of us. But she just kept screaming at me, 'You were going to kill my baby! You were going to kill my baby!' I left. That was in the last of December. I tried to call her several times, but she refused to take my calls at her home or at her office. The next time I saw her was a month later on Law Day in Two Harbors down in Lake County. She was as cold as a fish and still is. It isn't your car. I am the reason she wouldn't ride down to Duluth with you. I was going to be along."

Gregory sat in silence.

After a bit, Errol Joyce said, "Now she says she isn't going to put my name on the birth certificate as the father."

"You can't force her to?"

"I don't know. I never had a client who ever tried to. Have you?"

P.M. shook his head.

P. M. Gregory drove the dirty yellow Buick along the shore road from Grand Marais to the twin ports of Duluth and Superior, Wisconsin. The highway took them past the magnificent palisades that shielded the Arrowhead Coast. Highway 61 hugs the North Shore of the lake for one hundred forty miles until it reaches the mariner's town of Two Harbors. There the road becomes a divided expressway that is cut through stands of birch and aspen to the edge of the City of Duluth. Most of the route is rugged and rocky and runs through wooded sections of high bluffs, past gravel beaches famous for their yield of agates and other gemstones. Rivers spill from the south slope of the wilderness and flow under bridges and culverts into the fresh water of the lake.

After he was elected to the bench, Gregory turned his North Shore practice over to a young Errol Joyce. Upon his retirement, the old man returned to office in one room of Errol's building.

As if just remembering, P.M. Gregory pounded on the steering wheel and blurted out a story about the theft of his canoe.

"It was there beside the driveway where I unloaded it last night, and it's gone this morning. The paddles were out of sight under a bush or they would have taken them too," he speculated.

Joyce interrupted his friend. "I've got to find the missing twin."

Judge Gregory's mind lapsed into the past. He recalled his first encounter with the two Indian girls the summer after their father, Anton Saulturs, left their mother. The mother and her girls had reorganized their lives and for a holiday attended the Powwow and Rendezvous gathering at the Grand Portage Stockade. While the judge was talking to Marie Saulturs, Zona came darting through the crowd and called to her sister.

"Come on, Nina, they're going to have a canoe race."

Zona jumped with excitement. "They're going to have a race for kids," she said. "We haven't been canoeing all summer but I know we can win."

Nina pulled back and shook her head sharply. The judge had seen the girl's face tighten as she looked to her mother.

"Come on. We can win." Zona shook her sister's arm.

Judge Gregory watched Nina pull loose and back away. "I don't want to get in a canoe," she said.

Zona looked puzzled.

Nina winced, "I don't want to get in a canoe." As she turned to her mother, P.M. heard the girl add, "Not with you."

"Why would Nina run off?" asked Gregory.

"That's just a story that they're telling down in Duluth. Maybe she didn't run off," replied Errol.

"How did Zona die?"

"The news report was rather sketchy," said Joyce. " According to the police she was suffocated and then some sort of acid chemical was poured over her face to disfigure her. I don't know how the police arrived at chemicals being forced down the dead girl's throat. They have pretty good reason to believe that she was killed somewhere else, and her body was brought back to the dormitory."

"That doesn't sound right to me," said the old lawyer.

"Me neither," said Joyce, "but that's what they were reporting on the television."

As Errol Joyce and P.M. Gregory rode down the shore highway, they exhausted their speculation about the tragic events reported on the morning news and turned their attention to Errol's Indian trial.

"Can you get a Summary Judgment for Marie Saulturs from Judge Clemens?" P.M. asked.

"Probably not," admitted Joyce. "Engel Tormudson has filed his lawsuit against Marie Saulturs in her capacity as chief of the Ojibwa band and as the chief executive officer of both the hotel corporation and the Wedgewood-Ben Truck Line. Tormudson is trying to get Judge Clemens to remove Marie from her position on the theory that she is in violation of her fiduciary duties. He's asked for a trustee to be appointed in her place until there can be new tribal elections."

"Can't you argue that the jurisdiction is with the Federal Government instead of the State on the theory that the Bureau of Indian Affairs oversees tribal disputes and get the case thrown out of court that way?"

"I'm not worried about Marie's position as chief of the tribe," said Joyce. "You're right about federal jurisdiction in strictly tribal matters, but we set up the two Minnesota corporations to shelter the hotel and the truck line. The affairs of the hotel and truck line are administered by nine directors who are also members of the tribal council who own all the shares of stock in the two corporations. When the tribe bought the truck line, we leveraged the equity the tribe had in the hotel corporation by pledging the hotel stock to secure the loans of the truck line. Under Minnesota's Blue Sky Securities laws, Judge Clemens permitted the State to intervene to protect the interest of the public. That's why Jan Kiel with the Attorney General's regional office down at Duluth is involved."

"What interest of the public?"

"I set up the two companies under Minnesota's General Business Corporation Act," said Joyce. "All of the stock in both corporations are held by the Ojibwa band. The tribe could make an offer of sale of the stock to other Native Americans tomorrow. That was the basis of Judge Clemens' ruling that allowed the State to intervene."

"So you're going to have to go on with your hearing tomorrow," mused Gregory, "and you're going to have to have witnesses."

"Right," said Errol.

"Dorothy will probably give you a continuance if you ask for it in view of what's happened in Marie's family."

"I know that," said Joyce, "but the tribe can't stand a delay. While the stock in these two companies is tied up in litigation between tribe members, time will run out on the default provisions of the financing documents."

"How so?"

"When we financed the purchase of the truck line and pledged the credit of the hotel, the contract terms required there be no change in management without the consent of the mortgage holders. Otherwise the debt is accelerated, and all of it becomes due and payable."

"Even if management is changed by court order?" asked P.M.

"That's what the contracts say," replied Joyce. "The lenders contended they were entitled to deal with the management with whom they negotiated the loans or else call in the security. The tribe or Judge Clemens can order a change in the management team, but if they do, then under the terms of the loan papers, they will have to pay off the whole debt. That means the hotel and truck line will be foreclosed and lost. And, if there is a delay, the judge will appoint a temporary trustee, and even a court appointed trustee will trigger the default provisions of the loan documents."

"Doesn't Engel Tormudson know that?" asked P.M.

"Yes," nodded Errol Joyce, "but he's stubborn enough to think he can negotiate new terms with the lenders if he gets control of the corporations."

"Could he?"

"Those Wall-Street types can smell blood like a timber wolf. They wouldn't pass up the opportunity to get their hands on the tribe's assets. They would charge Tormudson a new interest rate that would wipe out the tribe's equity in two years."

"This intra-tribal fighting can ruin the Ojibwa band," said P.M.

"I agree," said Joyce. "I agree but there's nothing I can do about it except win the case for Marie and keep the management team as it is."

"Is Peter Hauck going to represent Engel Tormudson?" asked the old judge.

"I think so," said Joyce. "Engel told Judge Clemens that he changed his mind about representing himself. He said he would have Peter Hauck in the courtroom for tomorrow's hearing."

"I always did think Engel Tormudson had more sense than to try to be his own lawyer. When a man represents himself in court, he's got a damn fool for a client," growled P.M. Gregory.

Errol Joyce shrugged. "Engel has a lot of smarts. In any event, he told the judge that he was going to get in touch with Peter and have him in Grand Marais for the hearing tomorrow."

"What are you going to do about the girl's mother?" asked P.M. "You need her testimony at your hearing. With her daughter being murdered, she's not going to be in any frame of mind to litigate with other members of the tribe over who controls the hotel and truck line."

"I don't know," said Joyce. "I'll just have to wait and see what she says."

CHAPTER NINE

The Duluth Chapter of the University of Minnesota Alumni Association holds its fund-raising luncheon at the Radisson Hotel in downtown Duluth. The hotel is constructed in the round with rooms that spiral above the harbor where the St. Louis River flows into the most western tip of Lake Superior. To the north, stone and wood homes of the city spreads up the steep mountainside to spectacular Skyline Drive. The brownstone business district lies to the east. Interstate Highway 35 winds west, breaching the Masabe Range where the freeway meets the westernmost end of Skyline Drive. The windows of the meeting room on the top floor of the hotel presented those in attendance at the alumni meeting with a panorama of ocean-going vessels resting beside deep water wharves and blocks of grain elevators. In the distance, the flat lands beyond the City of Superior, Wisconsin stretches south to the horizon.

The Honorable Dorothy Lee Clemens, Judge of the District Court for northeastern Minnesota, and Assistant Attorney General Jan Kiel, who represented the State of Minnesota in its northern counties, were active collegiate alumni. While the University's Vice President in charge of Development was speaking, Jan tried to get the attention of Judge Clemens. When she did, the two women whispered excuses and went into the hallway where they could talk in private.

"Did you hear about Errol's client?" asked the Assistant Attorney General.

Judge Clemens shook her head.

"The girl who was found dead in the college dormitory is the daughter of Errol's client in the hearing you have scheduled for us in Grand Marais tomorrow."

"She was?" The lawyer's announcement startled the woman.

Jan Kiel nodded.

"Marie Saulturs' daughter?" asked the judge.

Again Jan nodded. "According to the reports that my office got before I left to come down here to the hotel, the dead girl hasn't been positively identified, but they believe that she is one of the twins, and the other twin is missing."

"I didn't know Marie Saulturs had twin daughters," said Judge Clemens.

"Yes," said Jan. "They are two very bright girls. They had finished their first year in college and were starting their sophomore year in this summer's session."

"Have you heard from Errol Joyce?" asked Judge Clemens.

"No," said Jan, "but I expect we will. If he asks for a continuance of tomorrow's hearing, I want you to know that the State will agree to a continuance."

"Did you ever hear whether or not the plaintiff, Engel Tormudson, was able to hire Peter Hauck to represent him?"

"The last I heard is what he said in court - he said he was going to try to get Peter to be his lawyer, but that's all I know," said Jan. "Nobody has contacted me saying he represents Tormudson."

"The hearing is set for eight-thirty tomorrow morning in the Cook County Courthouse," said the judge. "For now I'll leave the trial setting as it is. I don't know how to get hold of the plaintiff until tomorrow even if Errol asks for a continuance."

"I thought you should know about it in the event you hadn't heard the news or made the connection between the murder and Errol's client," said Jan.

The judge nodded sadly. "Horrible, just horrible" she breathed.

CHAPTER TEN

Next to the fire, in the camp of lawyer Peter Hauck, amid moss covered rocks and a clump of trees, Engel Tormudson straddled a large log and between his knees balanced a pan of hot fish and fried potatoes. The fire was a low bed of smoking coals under a black grille. The Indian looked about him. He thought the canoe party was traveling with too much gear. Hauck had brought along a camp box set on legs to serve as a camp kitchen, and there were two folding canvas chairs. Across the clearing, a large tent supported by ropes was tied to tree trunks and sagged in a patch of sunlight. Duluth packs, a wood saw and axe, life preservers, and several kinds of fishing gear were strewn across the clearing. A suitcase looking ridiculously out of place sat on the ground beside the entrance to the tent. The lawyer had chosen for his camp a flat shelf of rock that rose from the edge of the lake and lay among a stand of majestic Norway pines that spread a lofty canopy.

It was noon, and Engel was surprised to see that Hauck had made no preparation to move off his campsite. None of the gear was packed for their journey to the courthouse in Grand Marais.

"Just in time to eat," the lawyer had called from the fire when he saw Tormudson pushing his canoe into the rocky shore. Peter waved him up to the camp. Without ceremony Hauck filled a plate with fish and potatoes and handed it to Tormudson as the lawyer's greeting to his client.

Engel had chosen the fallen log for his bench and table.

Peter Hauck turned and called toward the tent. "We've got company. You better get out here, he's eating your breakfast!"

The lawyer grinned at the Indian. Engel had been told that the former law professor was seventy years old. He hadn't expected to find a man who looked to be forty.

"I went fishing his morning while Terry slept in," Peter explained. "I was cooking her breakfast when you arrived, but there is plenty more." Peter wiped his hand on his khaki jacket. Engel saw his woolen pants were wet to the knees. Under the jacket Peter wore a heavy red flannel shirt. Casting flies were hooked in a row to the band of the man's wide brimmed hat. The hat didn't quite cover all of his salt and peppered gray hair. Peter Hauck was a big man, congenial and shrewd.

"You're Engel Tormudson!" The lawyer reached over and shook Tormudson's hand. The Indian caught his sliding plate and nodded. He continued to appraise the Duluth lawyer he had hired unseen. The two talked on the telephone, but their meeting on the shore of North Lake was their first encounter. Despite the other's cordiality, Tormudson knew that he was also being studied. Their attorney-client relationship was still tentative.

"Terry!" the lawyer again turned and called.

Engel glanced at the tent opening and saw a woman step

out from under its canvass. The Indian stared, his spoon poised in mid air.

"Mr. Tormudson, this is Terry Whitehall-Banning," introduced Peter Hauck with a flourish. "My niece," he added.

The woman's clear, blue eyes were bright and opened wide. A smile lit up her face. She was stunning. More so even than Marie Saulturs, thought Tormudson, although he allowed that was probably because the woman at the tent was fifteen, perhaps twenty years younger than the Ojibwa leader. Also, she was taller than Marie, but no slimmer. Her silken brown hair, braided into a ponytail, hung to the middle of her back.

Slowly Tormudson placed his spoon on his plate. "Hello," he said. Engel didn't rise off the log. He continued to stare at the figure before him.

The woman was draped in a delicate black negligee. Engel had seen filmy gowns like hers before in magazines, but never on a live person. The delicate lace and its strategically-placed black panels were held up by narrow spaghetti straps. The gown had a neckline that opened most of the way down to her waist. There was a split in the side along her leg from hem to thigh. But what arrested the eyes of the Indian was the way the woman's beauty showed despite the gray suit of thermal underwear that covered her arms and extended from throat to ankle, underneath the diaphanous gown. Terry Whitehall-Banning wore a pair of hiking boots with laces that dragged the ground as she walked.

"I'm pleased to meet you, Mr. Tormudson," smiled the woman.

"I'm pleased to meet you," breathed the Indian.

Terry stepped past him and put her arms around the neck of the lawyer. She kissed him fully on the lips. Then, with a grin, the woman picked a roll of toilet paper out of the camp box and set off for the woods. "I'll be right back," she called over her shoulder.

Engel Tormudson choked. Wood smoke from the campfire burned his eyes. He set aside his plate. "You say she's your niece?" he asked wiping his face.

"My wife's," corrected Peter. He appeared to enjoy the Indian's apparent discomfort. "She's the daughter of my wife's sister. I guess that means she's my niece, too."

"Are you two up here alone?" asked Engel.

"Yeah," grinned the older man, "does that shock you?"

"Why should it?" challenged Tormudson.

"Well," said Peter, sitting down on the log, "I have to admit I'm old enough to be her father."

"Or, grandfather," interjected the Indian.

"Or, grandfather," admitted Peter Hauck. "She makes me feel young," said the lawyer. "She's my personal secretary, now," he explained, "everywhere I go she goes."

"What does your wife think about that?" asked Engel.

"I don't know," laughed the lawyer, "I never asked her."

Engel Tormudson picked up his plate. "Uncle and niece," he thought, "these two are no different than Marie Saulturs and Tom Boushey, the tribe's notorious first cousins." The man experienced a flush of jealously at the thought, the sensation that Engel always interpreted to be indignation.

Terry Whitehall-Banning announced that she was going to bathe in the lake. Peter and Engel watched the girl's slim figure disappear behind rocks at the water's edge.

"Ok," said the professor, "let's talk about your lawsuit."

"I filed it in Grand Marais," said the Indian, turning to do business.

"Why did you wait so long to call me?" asked Hauck.

"I thought I could handle it myself. I had a year of law school in Chicago," said Engel.

"You probably learned just enough law to get yourself into trouble. Why did you quit?" asked Peter.

"I ran out of money after my first year," replied the Indian.

"That's a good reason for quitting," admitted Peter Hauck. "Your suit is a Quo Warranto action?" he asked.

Engel Tormudson nodded. "I filed suit to ask the Court to enter an order enjoining Marie Saulturs from acting as chief of the band and as chairman of the tribal council."

"Did you bring up your file as I requested?"

From his pack the Indian produced a manila folder and handed it to Hauck.

The lawyer sat on the log and leafed through the documents, turning the pages and scanning their contents, sometimes turning back to re-read. After minutes of silence, Engel inquired, "Are you going to work for me?"

"No," Peter Hauck's smile was almost forced. "I work for myself," said the lawyer. "However, I will represent you."

The Indian nodded. "Represent me," he repeated.

The lawyer turned back to the papers. "Do you have witnesses to prove this?" he asked tapping the file.

"I do," said Tormudson.

"When you boil it all down," said Hauck, closing the folder, "you are accusing the chief of your tribe of using the Treaty of La Pointe rather than the regulations of the Bureau of Indian Affairs as the authority for spending tribal funds."

Engel nodded. "She claims the money she has spent on the hotel and the truck line was spent in accordance with power granted in the treaty, but it's not. She has ignored the federal regulations."

"Are you saying Marie Saulturs has embezzled tribal funds?"

"No, I'm not saying that. I'm saying she had no authority to divert tribal funds to the two private Minnesota corporations."

"Do federal regulations forbid that?"

"You're the lawyer," reminded Tormudson, "but my research shows that unless she can convince the court that she has some authorization, then her actions are ultra vires, beyond her powers. She's the one who violated her fiduciary responsibility. That means she must give up her office as chief of the band. There must be a new election."

"I see here," said Hauck tapping the file, "that Errol Joyce has filed an Answer saying that the Treaty of La Pointe gives Marie Saulturs broad authority to act as she did. He contends that the courts cannot interfere with that treaty."

"That's what he says," agreed Engel, "but I've subpoenaed a government official from the Bureau of Indian Affairs in Washington to prove that that's not so."

"Joyce is no dummy," said Hauck. "He has evidence to support his argument, or he wouldn't make it," offered the lawyer.

Engel Tormudson didn't answer.

"I also see that Jan Kiel, the Assistant Attorney General, has filed a pleading on behalf of the State of Minnesota. What's the State's interest?"

"The hotel and the Wedgewood-Ben Truck Line are public corporations. The State entered its appearance to protect the public interest in the event Marie Saulturs makes public offerings of the stock outside the tribe."

"Do you have a copy of the Treaty of La Pointe?" asked the lawyer.

"You missed it. It's in the very front," indicated the Indian.

Peter did not reopen the file. He did not take time to read the treaty which the United States Government made with the Chippewas in 1854.

Terry Whitehall-Banning came back to the campsite. Her nude body was covered and shivering in a large bath towel.

"Massage?" she asked as she brushed past Peter Hauck.

"Only a few more moments," promised Peter. She disappeared inside the tent.

The lawyer rose.

"I'll read the file tonight, and I'll meet you at the courthouse in the morning," he said.

Engel Tormudson didn't move from the log.

"Do you want to ask me any questions?" queried the Indian.

"Tomorrow," said Hauck. "I want to study the treaty. You know what you're going to say on the witness stand. No need for me to coach you."

Tormudson rose and looked darkly toward the tent.

Peter Hauck grinned. "Don't worry," he said. "You go back down to Grand Marais. We'll be along later. You get Terry and me a room at the Harbor Inn. Tell them to hold it for late arrival. Don't worry," he repeated, "I'll be prepared."

The lawyer leaned over to the Indian and inclined his head toward the entrance to the tent.

"She likes to have her feet massaged," he confided.

CHAPTER ELEVEN

In the gray basement room of Duluth Memorial Hospital, a room where one would expect to find the dead, thought Tom Boushey, a morose and uncommunicative police officer left a knot of people in gray cotton uniforms and approached Marie Saulturs and her companion. Beyond the group on the other side of the room was a white, partially open meat locker door, which poured frosty air through its opening. Tom and Marie felt its clammy cold. The officer who walked to them was not in uniform. He produced a badge of identification.

Marie removed her glove and shook the detective's hand. Tom also acknowledged the officer's greeting.

"I do not believe the dead person you have here is my daughter," the Indian mother spoke softly. She repeated the same statement of conviction that she had made to the law official upstairs.

"You're quite right," muttered the officer, putting his identification badge back in his pocket. He didn't look at the mother when he spoke. "The victim is not your daughter."

"Then why did the police say that she was?" asked the Indian woman. The man's face was marked with old pox scars but appeared intelligent enough, thought Tom. Marie couldn't tell whether it was cynical perversity, or simple distraction, that made the detective talk in the distant, impersonal way that he did. She knew of no reason why it should be either. "Perhaps," she thought, "he has been too long in his job and has dealt with too many homicides."

The detective shook his head. "The Police Department never did say the victim was your daughter. The only statement made by any member of our department was that the victim was found in your daughter's bed."

"That's not the way it was reported on television," said the woman.

"I'm sorry," said the detective, "but we do not have any control over media reports." Marie didn't think the man sounded sorry.

"Who was the dead woman?" asked the mother.

"I'm not at liberty to say," replied the officer.

"But you do know who she is?" asked Tom Boushey.

"I'm not at liberty to say," he repeated.

"If you knew that it was not my daughter, why did you ask me to come down to Duluth to identify the body?" asked Marie.

"You were asked to come down to Duluth but not for the purpose of identifying the victim's body."

"Then why?" The group across the room had stopped talking and was staring at her.

"We want to know if you can give us information as to the whereabouts of your two daughters."

"Zona and Nina?" asked the mother.

The detective nodded.

"Why?" she asked again.

"Just a part of the investigation," evaded the officer.

"No, it's more than that," said Marie. "Why did you summon me all the way down to Duluth to ask me about Zona and Nina?"

The detective looked past Marie when he talked. When he answered the mother's question, he chose his words carefully. "We have reason to believe that your daughters may be of help to us in completing our investigation."

"Are you saying my daughters have something to do with the woman's death?"

"I'm simply saying," repeated the detective, "that we have reason to believe that your daughters can be of help in solving this murder."

"Why?" asked Marie. "What makes you think Nina or Zona were involved in the woman's death?"

"Well, Mrs. Saulturs," said the officer, "the victim was found in the room your daughters shared in the dormitory and was found lying dead in the bed of one of your daughters."

"That doesn't mean my girls had anything to do with the woman's death," said Marie.

"That's why we want to talk with them," said the lawman, "to see what they have to say."

Tom Boushey spoke up. He eyed the gloomy detective curiously. "There's more to this than just finding the woman's body in the twins' room, isn't there?" He watched the officer closely.

The detective dropped his head. "I can't comment on that, Mr. Boushey. I'm only trying to find out where the two girls are. We have reason to believe they are material witnesses."

"Only witnesses?" asked Boushey.

"For now, yes - only witnesses."

"I don't like the tone of that," said Marie. "When you say 'for now' that sounds sinister to me."

"I'm sorry," said the detective.

For the first time since he confronted them he looked directly at Marie. "I didn't mean for it to sound sinister, but the only leads we have - the only suspects we have in the case - are your daughters. We are trying to find out where they are so we can question them."

"Have you inquired over at the college?" asked Tom.

The detective nodded, "We have. We've also made inquiry at the bus station, the airport, and," he added, "we've given their descriptions to the customs authorities at the Pigeon River border crossing and the border crossing at International Falls."

"Then you do suspect my daughters to be responsible for the death of this woman," said Marie.

"I've said nothing of the sort," replied the lawman. "I'm just simply trying to find out from you if you've seen your daughters, and I've alerted other authorities that we are looking for your daughters. They very well may have been taken from the campus against their will rather than to have run off."

"Or," interrupted Tom Boushey, "they may have just gone off for a visit. Students do that, you know," he reminded the detective.

The man nodded. "But in any event, I want to talk to them, and I have alerted other law officials to pick them up if they are found so they can be returned for questioning. I'm asking you to keep me informed if either of them make contact with you."

Marie looked over at Tom Boushey and then back at the detective. She nodded stiffly and pulled on her glove.

"Is that all?" she asked.

"Yes ma'am."

"And you don't need me to look at the body?" asked the woman.

"No." The man shook his head. "Even if you knew the dead woman, I doubt that you would be able to recognize her."

Marie lifted her chin then turned and walked back to the staircase.

"Call me, Mrs. Saulturs," said the detective. "If you hear from your daughters, call me."

CHAPTER TWELVE

Downstream, where the muddy portage trail bent away from the roar of the river, Yellow Fox stepped on a flat slab and felt the rock beneath his foot twist and give way. The Indian's face didn't change its wooden expression as he fell backward and slid down the rocky embankment. The dangling traps drug on the ground and tore loose from his backpack. As he continued to slide, the old man thrust both feet forward to regain his footing by digging in the heels of his moccasins and stopped his fall on a rock outcropping scarcely twenty feet from a clump of birch where the deserter, Axel Denek, lay hiding. The rusted traps came clattering down on the rocky ledge beside him.

Denek was startled when the old Indian lost his foothold, fell from the trail, and landed before him. The unnerved white man clutched the wooden paddles that he still possessed and pressed his body into the bed of moss that overgrew the forest floor.

When Axel heard the approach of the old Indian on the trail above him, the white man knew that he had run in full circle. At first, in his escape, Denek had veered away from the portage trail, but he re-crossed the path at a place where an opening was cut by a small stream. Axel followed the wet creek bed in search of a clean pool of water where he could drink and rest. Panic had guided the white man to the clump of trees, and he lay trying to collect his thoughts when the form of the old Indian crashed down to the rock ledge in front of him. Scarcely daring to breathe, Denek pressed his body into the bed of moss.

At first Yellow Fox lay on his back, raised his two hands and made fists. He flexed his stiff fingers. Then the Indian arched his back and tentatively moved his legs, the way elderly men do to test themselves before making an effort to rise. The old Indian looked fatigued, but he appeared to Denek to be uninjured by the fall. Yellow Fox, a short muscular man, his hair mostly black, his skin pale as sand, thick and rough, sat upright on the rock ledge. Reaching out, the Ojibwa secured the tangled ugly traps without rising. His back was close enough that Axel could almost touch the quills on the Indian's leggings.

The white man's fear began to flood and become submerged, displaced by bitter rage and humiliation. "The old Indian made a fool out of me in front of the girls," Axel again thought bitterly, and within him an irrational hatred began to build.

Yellow Fox was oblivious to the still form lying in the stand of trees behind him. With his stiff fingers, the old Indian set about to adjust the pouch and retie the leather thongs that held the metal traps to the side of the pack.

As Denek stared at the unprotected back of Yellow Fox, the veneer of pretense peeled away from his face. His boyish good looks faded into features that were pinched and eyes that were shrewd and sinister. Axel Denek knew that he was no coward, but he also knew how to calculate odds, and Axel was not the kind who would pass up an advantage.

The white man eyed the shotgun that lay on the ground beside the Indian. Despite the nearness, Denek doubted that he could seize the gun before the old man could turn on him.

Opposite his chin, Axel saw another weapon. A rock the size of a soccer ball lay in the moss where it had fallen from the ledge above the aspens. Mostly the rock was round, but one side was flat giving it a sharp, jagged surface.

Stealthily Denek rolled to his knees and reached for the broken piece of granite. Silently he cradled it in his hands and rose to his feet. With animal-like caution, Denek stepped behind the engrossed Indian. The white man stretched to his full height, and lifting the stone above his head, brought it down on the back of the neck of the old man.

Denek seized the gun and pointed it at the prostrate form, but the Indian had fallen without an outcry and lay without moving. A rasping sound from the old man's throat warned Axel that the Indian was still alive.

The white man stepped over to the body. He put the toe of his shoe under the Indian's chin and pulled it back so his neck was stretched. Balancing himself, Axel placed his foot on Yellow Fox's neck. Then, raising his other foot off the ground, he brought his full weight to bear on the man's throat. He saw the Indian's eyes open wide and bulge. Using the gun as a cane for support, Axel jumped twice. The neck bones snapped. The body convulsed. Axel Denek lost balance and, falling, slammed the gun's barrel onto the rock ledge.

"Damn!" muttered the white man. The long gun had bent, and he saw the damage to the metal had made the weapon useless.

Axel rolled onto his side and kicked the headdress away. As he crawled to his feet, he smelled a stench. The Indian's dead body released its urine and fouled the air with the same smell Axel had released at the clearing when the old man held

Denek's hand in his trap.

"I got you, you son-of-a-bitch," said Axel bitterly, "and it's too late for anyone to cut off their finger and ransom you!"

CHAPTER THIRTEEN

The morning breeze stopped. Vapors began to rise from the mud in the wet portage clearing. Insects swarmed through damp wood smells that saturated the air and seeped into the senses. The two Indian girls slapped at the mosquitoes and waited. Nina, seated on the overturned canoe, and Zona, stalking back and forth; both searching the rock bluff above them.

In exasperation, the pacing sister turned. "I don't see him. I don't know where in the hell he can be."

"He may be lost," Nina spoke fearfully.

"I hope he is," said Zona. She walked over to the canoe and stood in front of her sister. "I hope he wanders around on the rocks up there and falls and breaks his leg."

Nina shook her head, "Zona, you don't mean that."

Her sister put her hands to her hips. She said with disgust, "Nina, do you realize that man was willing to have someone cut off one of your fingers, rather than take the blame for stealing those paddles?"

"I heard what he said," the twin's tone was subdued, "but Axel knows nothing about this wilderness country. He is liable to wander off and fall through the moss covering. If he does, we may never find him."

Both knew the broken and treacherous rock formation with its voids and traps was the chief reason travel in the Boundary Water country is by canoe until winter freeze makes snow packed trails safe to travel by foot or snowmobile. Rarely did anyone try to hike the forest floor from early spring to late fall, except on ancient and tested portages between the lakes. Inland the terrain was a jumble of tree stands and massive, broken plates of lava rock, some as large as houses, fitted together irregularly after thousands of years of freeze and thaw, hidden by nature's woven carpet of moss and dense overgrowth. It was land reverenced, not feared, by the girls. Their mother had repeated to Zona and Nina the "river of words" taught all Ojibwa children that explained the mysteries of those things that were emblematical or symbolic to the Chippawa band. Their Indian heritage taught the Indian girls that the trees, with their shallow root system that held to rocks, are "emblems of life". "Like trees," they were taught, " you grow up, and like trees you pass away again." The dense forest and its dangers underfoot are not a menace for the North American Chippewa that it is for others.

"Are you telling me that you still care about Axel Denek after what he did?" Zona asked indignantly.

Nina ignored her question. "I just don't think that we should leave anyone out here in the woods who doesn't know what he's doing. Axel knows nothing about how to survive out here. We should try to find him. But," added Nina with a gesture, "we must do something with this canoe."

"The canoe will be all right where it is," said Zona.

"No," replied Nina. "Yellow Fox may come back and carry it off if he thinks we have abandoned it. Axel's secret formula is in it. You know what he did when we stopped down on the lake shore and he opened up the buoyancy chamber."

"We can't take the canoe with us," said Zona, looking across at the bluff on the other side of the clearing.

"Perhaps we can hide it," suggested Nina.

Zona looked around. The opposite side of their clearing was impossible to climb and also carry the burden of an eighty-pound canoe. Ahead of them she knew the swamp trail lead past the river's cascades to the abandoned site of Fort Charlotte. Behind them the three had crossed Grand Portage Creek, Popular Creek, and the mud and mire of the valley below Beaver Pond.

The famous pond had been mapped as a landmark on the Grand Portage trail for three centuries. By tacit agreement, trappers, voyagers, and Indians left the beaver colonies, which inhabited the impounded waters, undisturbed. The industry of the animals created, repaired, and when destroyed, rebuilt a woven wooden dam, sealing it with mud, holding back waters, and allowed travelers to avoid a nearly impassable ascent to the rock highlands that bordered the trail on the west. The beavers held the waters of the Pigeon River from the valley floor where, no matter how dry the season, an oozing mud trail was churned ankle deep by man and animals. The dam constantly leaked, sometimes overflowed, and on occasion the mudworks was breached by the turbulent river. When that happened, the valley flooded and blocked passage until the clever animals repaired their engineering marvel.

Zona instructed her sister. "Pick up that end of the canoe," she said. "I've got an idea what we can do with it." The girls grasped the thwarts of the craft and walked the canoe toward the bank of the river. At the edge of an area covered by moss, Zona signaled her sister to set the canoe on the turf. She tread the terrain cautiously, stomping her heel at intervals to test the forest floor.

"What are you looking for?" called Nina.

"One of the large lava tubes," answered Zona.

"Yes," agreed Nina, and she began exploring the footing under the wide bed of moss that lay along the bank of the river. She found a sharp stick and began thrusting it into the woven vegetation, pushing and twisting to find the opening between the large boulders that underlay the turf. It was Nina's probing stick that located a cave-like opening large enough to accommodate the canoe. "Over here," she called.

Cautiously Zona waded through the moss to the side of her sister. Nina punched with her stick several times to make a larger opening. Zona knelt and carefully began to lift clods of vegetation, an undergrowth that was tangled so tightly together it had grown a foot in depth. Carefully she broke off the chunks and made the opening large enough to permit her to peer inside. Satisfied that her sister had found a cave big enough to hold the canoe, she began to loosen the rest of the moss around the entrance and stack it at the edge.

"You need help?" asked Nina.

Zona shook her head, "No, stand still where you are so we will disturb the moss as little as possible." She put her hands on either side of the opening and peered into the dark shaft. Sunlight filtered inside and caused the black ceramic of the tube to glitter. Cocking her head, she could hear water sounds, like a distant open faucet. The tunnel appeared to be only slightly off horizontal. In its depth, Zona was certain it curled downward to reach the bed of the river, the source of the sound.

The Chippewa girl pushed herself to her feet. She and Nina lifted the canoe and carefully guided it into the opening. They slid it its full length.

Satisfied that the craft would not slip out of reach in the glass-like tunnel, the two girls retraced their steps to the muddy trail and walked several hundred feet before stepping off into the woods and breaking off branches. They stripped them for use as a woven brace to support the moss chunks they intended to replace to conceal the mouth of the tube. Again carefully stepping on the mossy turf, they carried their load of stripped branches to the lava tube. Using skills taught them by their mother, they wove a framework across the opening and positioned the moss chunks so that the dried foliage would match the rest of the bed's vegetation.

When the girls were satisfied the opening was camouflaged, they stepped backward across the turf and reached down to lift the crushed clumps of vegetation made by their footsteps. It took the two an hour to fully complete their task. Only the sharp eye of an experienced tracker would be able to discover what they had done, Zona thought.

"Yellow Fox can find it," said Nina.

"If he were looking for it," agreed Zona. "But if he comes back and finds the canoe gone, he'll think we have taken it with us, and that's just as well. I hope I never have to see him or speak to him again."

Zona led her sister back to the portage clearing where they had encountered the old Indian. She signaled for Nina to walk behind her, a distance the length of a canoe. The two girls carefully stomped into the oozing mud, tracks that gave the appearance that they were carrying a heavy burden. They marched along the trail as if to continue their journey toward the abandoned fort, and they kept up their charade until they reached the shelf of lava rock that rose out of the mud of the Grand Portage trail and provided a pathway past the cascades the last mile to Fort Charlotte.

Both girls sat on the rock and recovered their breath. They looked back down the trail and Zona nodded her head. "If Yellow Fox does come back, I think he will believe we picked up the canoe and continued on our journey," she said.

Nina lay back against the rock ledge behind her and looked across at her sister. "You didn't mean what you said about our father back there did you?"

"Yes I did," said Zona indignantly. "I would never have said it if I didn't mean it." Zona rolled on her side and looked back at Nina. "Don't you remember? Mother was bending over the sink crying, and he was standing there drunk in the middle of the kitchen floor with all that blood around him. You were crying too, but I asked where our dog was and he said for us to get out. Don't you remember that? He made us leave."

"Mother said he didn't kill our dog. She said he took our dog with him."

"She said that just so we wouldn't feel bad," said Zona. "Mother was there when he did it. He was drunk, and he killed our dog," insisted Zona.

"We said we wouldn't argue about this again," reminded Nina.

"You're the one who brought it up," said Zona. "He doesn't mean anything to me, he's not my father any more." The girl slid off the rock and stood up.

"Don't you think we should start looking for Axel?" Nina changed the subject.

"I suppose," said Zona. She looked down the muddy path. "If he has any sense at all, he will turn around and go back down the trail to the highway."

"He was so frightened when he ran toward the bluff," said Nina, "He may have missed the trail back to the highway."

"He won't go very far carrying those paddles," replied her sister. "And if I know Axel Denek, when Yellow Fox told him to take the paddles, Axel grabbed them so tightly he can't let them go."

Lurching to her feet, Nina said, "Come on Zona, let's see if we can find him."

The canoe was gone.

Axel Denek thrashed through the underbrush along the river until he reached impassable cascades and broken ridges of lava rock that forced him to turn back to the muddy trail of Grand

Portage. The white man was surprised to find tracks that led to the clearing where he had his encounter with Yellow Fox. Axel realized that he had again traveled in a circle.

"The girls didn't come back down the trail where I was," he reasoned. "They must be on up ahead, and they must have taken the canoe with them."

Denek secured at his waist the knife he had taken from the fallen Indian, concealed its handle with his jacket, and then followed the trail out of the clearing. He saw the footprints in the mud made by the girls and followed them to the shelf of rock where the twins had turned back. In his haste, Denek assumed the sisters had continued along the rock ledge toward the abandoned fort, so he hurried, intent on stopping the two women before going back and securing the paddles he had left behind.

The Indian girls retraced their steps to the clearing where they had last seen Denek, being careful to step into the holes their footprints had made in the mud. Zona took the lead in the search for Axel. "It's not difficult to follow him," she said. Nina agreed. The broken foliage and fresh overturned rocks showed the flight of the white man to the base of the bluff and the start of his climb. The trail led up and away from the clearing. It crested the top of the bluff and then led the girls down to a damp creek bed. Footprints indicated that Axel hesitated then turned to follow the flow of the creek that led him back toward the river and the churning waters of the cascades. For another half-hour, Zona and Nina tracked Axel. Once they stopped and examined impressions where he had knelt to drink from the stream. Several times they saw indented marks near his footprints in the soft wet mud.

"He still has the paddles," Nina pointed.

"I told you he would," said Zona. "He's too scared to let

them go."

"He needs the paddles to get across the border," said Nina. "Otherwise he wouldn't still have them."

The creek bed and Denek's footprints led them back across the portage trail. "The man is walking in a circle," thought Zona. The prints led down the trail as if the man intended to hike back to the state highway, but the girls saw a second set of impressions indicating that Axel had returned, crossed the trail at the creek, and turned toward the river.

"Wait," said Zona, she was puzzled by the man's move. "Let's go down the path and see why he did that."

The sisters followed the mud trail. After two hundred yards they came into sight of a sheet of water. The valley below the beaver dam was flooded, and the trail on which they were walking disappeared. Across the valley, they could see where the track of mud rose out of the water and continued its five-mile path south toward Lake Superior and the coastal highway.

"Where did the water come from?" Nina asked aloud.

Her sister pointed. "Something has caused a break in the beaver dam and the trail to flood."

"We're trapped up here," surmised Nina. "We can't get across the river without going above Fort Charlotte, and even then, we would have to use the canoe to get into Canada. This flooded valley won't let us go down to the state highway without the canoe either. We have no paddles."

"We can walk out if we must," said Zona, "and if we're careful," she added. "Let's go see where Axel went with those paddles."

The girls retraced their steps to the creek bed and followed Axel Denek's trail where it left the track and turned down toward the river.

"The paddles!" yelled an excited Nina. "I see the paddles. They're laying over there in the brush."

Zona, who was in front of her sister, had stopped, her face ashen white.

Nina stepped beside her. She looked down. Lying on the ground was a yellow scrap of fur, and beside it lay the broken body of the old Indian.

"Oh my God!" breathed Nina.

CHAPTER FOURTEEN

All Ojibwa children of a cabin, or lodge, regard the sisters of their mothers as their "sendove," their mother. They regard all the brothers of their fathers as their "agastan," their father. All the children on the side of the mother and her sisters; and the father and his brothers are regarded among themselves to be "atiquon" and " eadse," brothers and sisters. Tom Boushey and Marie Croche were reared as children of the same lodge, as "atiquon" and " eadse." But in white man's parlance, they were first cousins, and they were bound by the ancient Anishinabe taboos that forbid them to have children. A taboo for which death had been the penalty assessed by the old ones and for which being ostracized was the penalty of the modern Indian. The dangers of inbreeding were known, and feared, by the Anishinabe eons before white men set foot on the North American continent.

Engel Tormudson was a child of another lodge, withdrawn, quiet, and embarrassed by his taint of white blood. He had watched, with envy, Marie and Tom grow up to be lovers. It was birthing, not loving, that was forbidden. And, after the civil demonstrations on the Mandan Reservation, he saw Marie and Tom part; she to the University of Chicago and Tom to obtain a teaching certificate at Bemidiji State College, in Bemidiji, Minnesota.

Marie had wanted children. There were those in the tribe who said her marriage to Anton Saulturs, the peculiar college instructor from the tribe of the Plains Ojibwa, a Canadian national twenty years her senior, turned out to be a marriage of convenience. Marie's marriage to Anton had been a disappointment to Engel Tormudson as well as to Tom Boushey. There were those in the tribe who said that despite his position as a visiting instructor on the University of Chicago campus, Anton was ill suited for Marie, or for civilization; that Anton was both foe and kindred spirit to the animals of the forests. Those in the tribe who gossiped about such matters expressed surprise that Anton gave Marie the children that she wanted. The college instructor was an enigma, untamed, a follower of the water trails and the portages who matched wits with the cunning beasts that he hunted, and who hunted him. But they had married, and after Marie obtained her degrees, they returned to live on the reservation. Before the youngest child was born, Anton Saulturs took to living off the land, finally disappearing altogether. After college, Engel also married. Tom did not. The three, Marie, Tom, and Engel, worked together in the council to build the fortunes of the tribe, but they never spoke of young love.

However, Engel knew Marie had never changed her feelings for her cousin since the day, during their fourteenth summer, when Engel lay concealed on a mossy bluff and watched the "atiquon" and the "eadse" make love. That summer on a moss bed beside a blueberry patch above waters, whose islands shimmered and danced in bright sunlight, young Tormudson had watched as Tom spilled the entire contents of a sack of blueberries, the full length of the girl's body, and lay himself upon her, sliding back and forth while she clung to him, her mouth open, locked to his. He saw the mashed pulp and juices flow between them and the slow rhythmic movement as they ground the stained cloth of their underpants together, licking and biting until Engel felt his own skin go hot, then prickle, as if he had been too long in the sun. When he could not endure the scene any longer, Engel Tormudson slipped away. The emotion Engel experienced watching from the ledge that afternoon became an indignation that ever after was a part of his life.

Marie Saulturs and Tom Boushey stood at the rail on the wooden front porch of the new construction that housed the office of the Ojibwa tribal council. The unfinished building was erected at the edge of the Indian village. Although already used as her office, its wood siding was stacked beside the porch waiting to be nailed to the outer walls. The couple could see the rock shore of Lake Superior between slanted trunks of birch and aspen, black and gray trees, separated by the colors of their loose bark. Above the stand of trees, sometimes directly over their heads, sea gulls whirled, scolding, contesting, and skimming on spread wings, dirty white with smudged tips. Tiny brown and white forest birds, chirping a thin sound, announced to the Indian couple that they were also present.

"Do you intend to go on with the court hearing tomorrow?" Tom asked.

Marie nodded. "I think I should. The tribe has so much at risk," she said. "I'll worry about the kids, but I might just as well worry about them in the courthouse as here."

"Do the twins get along all right?" asked Tom. He deliberately tried to make his question sound casual.

"Yes," said Marie, "they do now."

"The girls haven't been very close though, have they?"

Marie looked up at Tom's long, narrow face, deeply seamed. She noticed his cheekbones remained as when they were children; pronounced, and he still had a sharp, clear chin. "No," she admitted.

"That has surprised me," said Tom. "Over the years I have noticed an estrangement, unusual for a pair of twins." Marie stared silently through the trees at the waters of the lake.

"Why did the twins fight the way they did when they were growing up?" asked Tom Boushey.

"They didn't fight any more than other children I suppose," said the mother without turning.

Tom shook his head, "I remember one time out in front of the reservation store when those girls were only eight years old. They got down and fought in the dust, screaming and pounding each other. I thought that Nina was going to pull the hair out of Zona's head. And," he asked, "do you know what they were fighting over?"

Marie shook her head.

"If they had been fighting over a boy, piece of clothing, or a toy, I could have understood that, but what they were fighting over was which one had loved their dead dog the most." Tom looked over at Marie. "When those two kids were growing up here in the reservation, they were twins only because you made them twins. If you hadn't made them cut their hair the same way and dress the same, a stranger would never believe that they were related."

Marie turned her head. Her expression was pained and troubled as she carefully chose her words. "It started, I think, the day Anton left. Zona and Nina were playing outside the cabin, and Nina fell off the bluff into the lake. She nearly drowned. Anton didn't think he was going to get her out of the water. He did, but he was so upset that he accused Zona of pushing Nina on purpose. I know Anton didn't mean it, but he was angry and went stalking off. The twins were different after that. Like they had a wall built between them, like they weren't even sisters. I never realized until the night of their high school graduation how bitter they were that I made them dress like twins." The mother brushed back a strand of her hair. "But when they went off to college, the three of us had a long talk, and the girls agreed to be roommates and to try to get to know one another. I think they got along better after they left home and went down to Cloquet."

Tom blew out his cheeks and cast his eyes up at the afternoon sun. He could feel the mother's anguish. "I'll go look for the girls," he said simply. "There has been so much radio publicity, Nina and Zona can't help but know that the police are searching for them."

"Nobody has located the car yet." Marie almost whispered her words.

Tom nodded and stared through the trees at the water. He spoke his thoughts aloud. "It wouldn't make any sense for the girls to just be hiding out. If they've left their car, then the reason the Honda hasn't been found is because it is hidden some place nearby, probably near the border crossing up at Grand Portage. Because if Nina and Zona are running away, they wouldn't go south to Minneapolis or St. Paul. They don't know those cities well enough to hide there. Up in Canada they would be beyond Minnesota authorities. That's where I think they are headed, into Ontario. The only highway crossings are here at Pigeon River or clear across the state at International Falls. If they're trying to get into Canada, they're not doing it at the patrolled highway crossings, they're doing it on foot or in a canoe." Tom nodded to Marie. "If I can locate the car," he knew he was guessing, "I can figure out the route Nina and Zona are taking to get into Canada."

"Grand Portage Stockade is having Rendezvous Days up at the Pigeon River with a large crowd of people," said Marie.

"A perfect place to hide a car," agreed Tom. "Three thousand visitors are up there for the celebration, and the girls know that."

Tom indicated to the telephone inside the office building.

"Marie, I think you should call and try to locate lawyer Joyce. He may be back from Duluth by now. If I find the girls, they shouldn't talk to the police until they first talk to Errol." Marie nodded. "You see if you can find the girls and I'll see if I can find Errol."

P.M. Gregory shook his head. "I don't understand, Errol. You say at your meeting that the Neville Company said for you to get their guy Faulks off before he is even charged in an arraignment? And if you don't get him off, the company is going to see that some harm comes to Jan Kiel and your baby?"

"The CEO, MacKenzie, said that."

"But you think he is bluffing? This man that heads up a powerful Canadian corporation makes a threat like that, and you have done nothing about it? Haven't talked to the police or discussed the threat with the judge who is going to try the case? You haven't even told Jan Kiel about the threat to harm her and your baby?"

"No." Errol shook his head. "I don't think it is necessary. I led the Neville Mines people to believe that I would take on their man's defense, but I only did that to stall for time while I figured this thing out."

"What's there to figure out? A company CEO threatens to harm your daughter and her mother unless you let yourself be blackmailed into defending their guy. I don't see anything for you to figure you. Go to the police! Tell the Attorney General down at St. Paul!"

"I don't want Jan to get upset this far into her pregnancy when it isn't necessary. You know she had that trouble early on when she got hurt at the ski lodge. Besides, MacKenzie is only bluffing."

"How do you know that he is only bluffing?"

"By the story he told about shooting people in Korea."

"He was over there wasn't he? It was wartime."

"Yes, but as an officer on the general staff! Something like that wouldn't happen without a scandal. And a big scandal. There would have been a ton of publicity, and I would have heard of it. No mention of anything like that was made when the Black Bear was dealing with Neville Mines at the time the company was trying to partner up with the Casino. Stories like that one about a shooting of defenseless Korean civilians would follow a person their entire career. I don't believe it happened, and I think he is just bluffing about harming Jan and the baby."

"Okay! Then why would he do that? Why would the CEO of a large corporation risk losing his company's credibility by telling such a story?" asked P.M.

"That is what I had to buy time for – to find out."

"And have you?"

Errol Joyce shook his head. "No. All I can figure is that this guy Faulks has something on the company or the chairman that they are afraid he will reveal if he is required to testify under oath at any kind of hearing."

"Such as what?"

"I don't know P.M. But if this Faulks guy realizes that if he tells lies under oath, he is guilty of not only contempt of court but also perjury, he may have told MacKenzie to get him off or if asked the right question, he would tell the truth rather than take a chance on being convicted of a perjury count."

"And what might that be?"

"Damn if I know. But I'm going to interview Faulks and find out."

"That will add to the mess. Faulks thinks you are his lawyer. You interview him, he tells you MacKenzie killed the girl and gave him the contents of her purse, or some such tale, then what do you do? Even if that were so, you can't tell the judge or the Attorney General. That is a confidential communication between attorney and client – you and Faulks. If you reveal what he has told you, you can lose your law license. And if you don't reveal what he tells you - if you don't tell Jan, she and your kid may be in real danger. You are still going to be on the other side of a criminal prosecution from Jan, unable to say anything to protect her."

For several minutes the two sat in silence studying the puzzle.

"And there is another thing too, Errol. If MacKenzie's threat is a bluff, then how did he get his hands on Jan Kiel's medical records? How did he get to see a picture of your kid to find out its sex? Without the mother's consent you couldn't get a copy of the ultrasound, how did he?"

Joyce shook is head. "I haven't figured that out yet."

"Until you do," P.M. said, "don't you think you should take MacKenzie's threat seriously?"

CHAPTER FIFTEEN

The North Shore at Grand Portage is a land of volcanic ridges that cuts across U.S. Highway 61 and pushes out into the lake forming rocky cliffs and protecting quiet coves. Here, there is a traditional gathering of several thousands for the region's annual Rendezvous and Powwow. The event is the occasion when Chippewa from across the Midwest and Canada assemble to dance the old dances and show off their ornate and delicately worked costumes. The annual Rendezvous also brings back costumed white men who outfit themselves in the seventeenth century dress of the Highland Scots who were partners and clerks of the North West Company.

The Indian schoolteacher, Tom Boushey, knew that technically the stockade is not part of the Thunder Bay Reservation. It is a national monument maintained by the National Park

Service. Within its palisade is the reconstructed Great Hall, where partners of the North West Company wrangled over the privilege of partnership and kitchen from which meals were served to those who enjoyed the Great Hall's privileges. Outside the gate, a canoe warehouse was reconstructed by the Park Service on the site of an independent trader, a competitor who later joined with the North West Company. A dock is built at the water's edge. It was from the water's edge at the Grand Portage that Alexander Mackenzie commenced his journey to the interior to find the Pacific Ocean ten years before the Lewis and Clark expedition.

Tom Boushey sat straight in the automobile and gathered his thoughts. A dampness rolled in from off the lake and made Tom's hair wilt against his cheek. The lake's breath of fog inched its way inland until it blurred Tom's view of the aspen and pine, except for the very closest tree trunk - the Witch Tree - on Hat Point across the shallow bay from the Grand Portage National Monument.

The girls had chosen an inconspicuous parking spot to hide their car, thought Boushey, a spot mostly surrounded by scrub underbrush. A breeze started blowing offshore to meet the moist, damp air from the lake and carried sounds of practice drums from the camp of the visitors who filled the valley, east of the wooden walls of the stockade. The brash sound of music from a radio also drifted across the bay.

The moon rose behind the small, twisted cedar tree that stood sentinel on Hat Point.

"The Witch Tree," thought Tom. "Nobody knows how it can grow like that in the cracks in the rocks. I should have thought of searching for the car here first."

Tom watched as the moon outlined the bare twisted trunk and cluster of top branches. "For four hundred years," thought the Indian, "our people who traveled by birch bark canoe, and later the French-Canadian voyageurs who came, offered tobacco at the base of Ma-ni-do Gee Zhi-gance, which in Ojibwa means 'spirited little cedar tree'. They made their offerings for their safe journey over dangerous waters. I should have guessed the girls might stop here."

Tom gazed reverently at nature's oddity. Waves lapped the rocks on the shore. Behind the Indian, along the mountain range to the north and west, occasional flashes of lightning glowed in clouds massing there.

Tom Boushey had searched throughout the afternoon. In the evening he inquired at the flickering campfires, but he found no trace of the Saulturs twins or of their car. He drove past long lines of parked vehicles, none belonged to Marie's daughters. It was after dark when he found the Honda parked near the Witch Tree and made his way to the public telephone to call the girls' mother.

"I've heard nothing from the police nor from the customs agents," responded Marie. "So the girls didn't try to drive the car across the border at Pigeon River before they abandoned it." The woman's voice sounded tired.

"They could still be here," Tom spoke into the telephone. "There's a big crowd, lots of cars, and it's dark. I think I'm going to have to give up for tonight and come back early tomorrow morning to see if I can find them."

"Yes," agreed Marie, "I don't think you can do any more up there tonight."

"I called hoping they had made contact with you," said Tom.

"No," replied Marie, "I haven't heard a word from them."

"Did you talk to Errol?"

"Finally," said the woman. "He thinks that he should be with the girls when they are questioned by the police, but we've also got the trial starting tomorrow down in Grand Marais."

"Do you still plan to go down to the trial, or stay up here tomorrow?" asked Boushey.

"Oh," sighed the voice at the other end of the line, "I told Errol I would be down at the courthouse in Grand Marais in the morning. I can do as much good down there as I can up here. I think the girls are all right. I have the feeling that they both can take care of themselves, but I don't want them to be scared and run off just because the police want to question them."

"There's nothing more I can do tonight up here," repeated Tom. "I'm going to come back tomorrow morning. If I get the girls found tomorrow, then I'll come on down to the courthouse where you're having the trial."

As the tall Indian walked back to his car, his thoughts were of Nina and Zona. He loved the twins as if they were his own daughters. Through the darkness Tom saw the rising moon. It still outlined the lonely Witch Tree on the cliff across the bay. He had seen the sight many times before, and it haunted him as it had haunted generations of his tribesmen. The Indian began to hum an ancient tribal prayer, a totem that would keep Marie's daughters safe from harm as they traveled the path that he could not find.

Errol Joyce sat in P.M. Gregory's one-room office.

"Well," Joyce said, "Marie and Tom think they know where the twins are now. Marie called me after I got back into town. She says the girls may be trying to go up into Canada. Tom has gone after them. I promised Marie that if they're found I will go down to Duluth and be there when the police question them."

"If Tom finds them, are you going to have time to do that? Your trial starts tomorrow."

"I might not," admitted Joyce.

"Then what?" asked the old man.

"Then you're going to have to go down to Duluth for me and represent the twins," said Joyce.

"Errol," said P.M., "I haven't handled the preliminary investigation of a criminal case in over thirty years."

"We're never too old to learn are we?" Errol Joyce smiled.

CHAPTER SIXTEEN

The sun broke through the horizon that divided azure sky and black rolling waters. The orb climbed through skeins of mist and fog over Lake Superior made golden with early morningrays. By eight o'clock it spread its brilliance to the lighthouse at the entrance of Grand Marais harbor, started warming the rocky beach at the town waterfront, and lighting the six concrete columns that rose from the courthouse steps three levels to the roof.

The Cook County Courthouse lay halfway up the side of the Sawtooth Range, a spectacular rampart which rose out of the harbor covered with aspen, birch, and pine.

Judge Dorothy Lee Clemens' courtroom occupied most of the third floor. Morning light reflected off the chamber's spotless glass windows that were opened to free the stale night air and let in refreshing early lake breezes. Yellow rays cast a glow that muted the alabaster ceilings and wainscoted walls. Sturdy oak furniture made up the judge's bench, the witness box, the rows of jurors' chairs, and the counsel tables inside the railing. Beyond the dividing rail, rows of spectator pews extended to the back of the room.

Despite the hour, the spectators' part of the courtroom was filled with silent, suspicious tribesmen and women from the Thunder Bay Reservation. Discordant neighbors, who chose sides on opposite benches, were split by the center aisle. All were in rough dress, mostly khaki or denim. The majority was men, but there were some women present, and discomfort was evident in all their faces.

The followers of Engel Tormudson sat closest to the doorway and hall. The followers of Marie Saulturs sat closest to the great windows.

Each newcomer that stepped into the courtroom surveyed the faces turned to the door, and after choosing made his way to the benches of the leader he supported. The women were predominantly young and were few, compared to the clutch of men who filled the seats and stood along the walls of the room. The women's conversation was low, muffled, a mixture of English, French, and Ojibwa. The men sat silent and acknowledged the presence of newcomers with only a somber nod.

Inside the railing, lawyers Errol Joyce and Jan Kiel sat at one of the counsel tables and watched Peter Hauck unload a stack of law books. The jury box was empty, as was the witness chair and the chair for Judge Clemens. However, the clerk of the court, the deputy sheriff, and the court reporter were in their places inside the railing with the attorneys.

Peter nodded a greeting to the other two lawyers. Behind him, beyond the railing on the first bench, two members of the Ojibwa band rose and stepped aside to make room for the slender figure of Terry Whitehall-Banning, who arrived dressed in a stunning white sweater and navy blue slacks. Her face was lit with child-like curiosity. She smiled in anticipation at

Peter, who returned her smile with a wink.

Errol's client sat at the counsel table beside him; hands folded in her lap. At the other table, Engel Tormudson's chair was beside Peter's. Engel was relieved to see his lawyer. The armload of books Peter had pulled from the shelves of the courthouse law library, the Indian thought, was a good sign.

There was a jostling at the entrance to the courtroom. A gray-haired woman carrying a bulky briefcase elbowed her way through the knot of men and came to the railing. Engel Tormudson rose and introduced his lawyer to the witness.

Errol watched. He had dealt with Ivella Zahn before. She was a woman Errol begrudgingly admired. Errol was aware of the subpoena Tormudson had issued, but he was disappointed that the Bureau had elected to interfere in the tribe's controversy by sending its deputy administrator to attend and testify. Joyce knew the Government could have claimed executive privilege and declined the state court subpoena. As he watched the three across the room, Errol realized he was going to try the lawsuit not only against Tormudson and his lawyer, but also against the United States Government, appearing by the Deputy Administrator, and against the State of Minnesota, who was represented by Assistant Attorney General, Jan Kiel. For the purpose of the trial, he knew his friend Jan sat at his counsel table as a matter of convenience. She was also the enemy.

Jan nudged Joyce. "Is that Peter's Washington witness?" she asked.

Errol nodded. "Yes, Dr. Zahn."

Ivella looked across at the second counsel table. She sat her briefcase outside the railing and stepped around the swinging gate. Ivella smiled and held out her hand.

"Hello, Marie," she said.

Marie Saulturs' face did not change expression. As she took the other woman's hand, Marie replied, "Hello, Ivella. I'm sorry to see that you have come."

Dr. Zahn continued to hold on to the Indian woman. "I'm

just doing my job, Marie."

Marie withdrew her hand. She did not answer.

Errol rose.

Dr. Zahn said, "It's good to see you again Errol."

The lawyer nodded. "It's good to see you too, Doctor." Turning, he made an introduction. "Dr. Zahn, this is Assistant Attorney General, Jan Kiel. Jan, this lady is Dr. Ivella Zahn, Deputy Director of the Bureau of Indian Affairs."

Jan rose and gripped the woman's hand. "I understood that Engel Tormudson had subpoenaed you to testify," she said.

Dr. Zahn shook her hand. "Not me. The subpoena was served on the Bureau, and I was selected to be the one to appear." Looking down at Marie, she added, "It wasn't my choice."

The door behind the judge's bench opened.

The deputy sheriff announced, "Everybody rise!"

Ivella Zahn retreated outside the railing and found room beside Terry Whitehall-Banning to stand as Judge Dorothy Clemens assumed her place at the bench and sounded her gavel.

"Please be seated," she announced.

CHAPTER SEVENTEEN

Above the town, giant rock cliffs, with jutting profiles, looked down their bony noses at the Cook County Courthouse. Trees posed on the skyline wore unkempt wigs, and their thin branches gestured resembling open arms. Below the courthouse, outside the breakwaters of the bay, the lake was like a giant's chest slowly heaving in great breaths of sleep, or walking in shivers of choppy waves. Soft swells bounced off the piers with an uneasy rise of its surface which seagulls rode snug.

Inside the courthouse, in the third floor courtroom, waiting brought a stillness.

There was a sense of mystery in the Native Americans, so rich in heritage, so rich with history. On their minds was the question: what is going to happen? All who had came down from the reservation anticipated the vivification of the Treaty of La Pointe. Some of the observers exchanged whispers, but most, like the lawyers seated inside the bar, remained silent and watched. The judge, a handsome woman, sat at her elevated bench with the case file before her, reading.

While he waited, Errol Joyce's eyes, most of the time narrow, swept the room taking in much and sending out little. The heavy witness chair beside the bench was on a raised platform, empty. Seated in front of the witness chair was a short fat balding man dressed in a snug suit. The lawyer's face twisted into a tight smile. "No one," he thought, "talks like our court reporter." His voice is patatoey, burred, and edgeless. For one skilled with the written word, Errol thought it a contradiction that the reporter's spoken consonants and vowels were indistinguishable. He noticed that the little man, who sat at his stenotype machine looking expectantly at the judge, again was wearing mismatched socks.

The jurist was petite, with auburn hair that appeared simply washed and worn naturally. Despite her forty plus years, she looked as young as her friend, Jan Kiel. Errol, like most of her constituents, knew that Dorothy had had a bad marriage, followed by a bad divorce, but she had no children. Clemens was Phi Beta Kappa and a member of Order of the Coif, an honors law society at the university. The North Shore community gossiped about the startlingly attractive woman's preference for young men, but by in large, her constituents agreed that her private life was her own affair. Most who met Dorothy Clemens took an instant liking to her, and those she confronted in the courtroom begrudgingly admitted that she was strict, but fair.

Shifting, Joyce scrutinized Peter and his client at the other counsel table. Engel Tormudson sat straight, one foot thrust in front of him, one tucked under his seat, as if preparing to stalk. There was a purposeful intent in the way he was seated. The law books Peter brought into the courtroom were stacked on the floor beside his chair; one volume lay with its pages open. Peter was bent over, reading a paragraph from the text without bothering to pick the book off the floor. Jan Kiel, Errol noted, had moved to the end of their counsel table and turned so she faced the judge. Jan shared the table with him and the quiet Ojibwa woman, but she distanced herself from them when Dorothy convened court. All waited for the judge to complete her reading.

Finally, looking up, Dorothy asked, "Is the Petitioner ready?" The whispers of the Indians outside the rail faded. The spectators stirred and settled in for the contest that was about to begin.

Peter Hauck rose and replied, "Yes, Your Honor."

The judge addressed Jan. "Are you appearing on behalf of the State of Minnesota?"

Jan rose. "Yes, Your Honor."

Errol Joyce also stood. "Your Honor, the Respondent is in the courtroom and ready for trial," he announced quietly.

"All right," said Judge Clemens. She pushed back the file and reached for a yellow pad. Joyce noted the woman was starting the proceedings with a handful of sharpened pencils. "It will be helpful to the court," she said, arranging them on her desk, "if the counsel for the Petitioner and the Respondent make brief opening statements of their client's version of the issues and of the evidence they expect to rely on to address their client's positions on those issues. Do the parties desire to make opening statements before the Court proceeds to hear the evidence?"

"Yes, Your Honor," said Peter Hauck.

"Yes ma'am," nodded Errol Joyce.

Jan Kiel replied, "The State does not propose to make an opening statement. The Attorney General has consented to the action however, the Petitioner's case will be presented by Mr. Tormudson's attorney."

"All right then," said Judge Clemens, her pencil poised, "the Petitioner may make his opening statement."

While the others took their seats, Peter walked around the

counsel table and stood in front of the empty jury box. Those outside the rail settled themselves and waited. Peter flashed a smile at the young woman on the front row and turned to address the bench.

"May it please the Court," he began. "The issues in this case are few and, by in large, the facts that will be presented are undisputed. This is an action in Quo Warranto. This is an action that asks the question 'by what authority does Marie Saulturs, the Respondent, act.' This is an action filed in the name of the State of Minnesota on behalf of my client, Engel Tormudson, for the removal of Marie Saulturs from the office of chief and the office of chairman of the tribal council of the Ojibwa band. The Petitioner charges that Marie Saulturs has acted without authority, in an ultra vires manner, by creating two private Minnesota corporations and transferring funds of the tribe into the treasury of those two corporations. My clients will prove to the Court that the actions of their chief have been outside the scope of her authority and, contrary to the rules and regulations of the Bureau of Indian Affairs, promulgated by the Bureau pursuant to federal law."

Like a liquid, the lawyer smoothly poured his words.

"It is the contention of the Petitioner," continued Peter Hauck, " that the District Court of the State of Minnesota has jurisdiction in this matter and has the authority to remove the Respondent from her office because the transfer of funds took place in the State of Minnesota and were deposited in the corporate account of two Minnesota corporations, which were created to build a hotel and convention center and to purchase, own, and operate a common carrier."

The man's voice was pleasant, confidential, and naturally pitched to hold everyone's attention. Indicating to the stack of books he had brought from the Cook County law library, Peter continued.

"The Petitioner will present to the Court previous decisions of our appellate courts that support the Petitioner's view that the issues here are properly State issues that have not been preempted by federal law; that the relief sought by this Petitioner can be granted by this Court. After hearing all of the evidence, the Petitioner believes that the Court will find that the chief of the Ojibwa Tribe, the chairman of its tribal council, has improperly transferred funds of the tribe into private corporations and should be removed from office, and a new election for chief and chairman of its tribal council should be ordered by this Court."

Peter's confident summary completed his statement. With a nod to the bench, he returned to his chair.

Judge Clemens turned to Errol Joyce.

Errol rose. "There will be no complaint raised in this proceeding of misappropriation of funds Your Honor." With commanding inflection, his tone took charge of the proceedings.

"The Respondent does not want the court to have the impression that any money has been stolen or improperly transferred to the accounts of any other person. The issues raised by the Petitioner, Engel Tormudson, have to do with his complaint that the tribal council, under the leadership of my client, voted to create two Minnesota corporations. The members of the tribal council, including the Petitioner, constitute the directorship of both of those corporations. This was done to meet the economic problems that exist up here in the Arrowhead Country, by constructing a hotel and convention center, and by purchasing the Wedgewood-Ben Truck Line to provide jobs for Native Americans who live on the reservation." The lawyer spoke to the central issue confronting the tribe.

"The evidence of the Respondent will be that the hotel has been constructed and is in operation. The common carrier, the Wedgewood-Ben Truck Line, has been acquired. As a result of these investments made by the tribal council, some ninety jobs have been made available to members of the Ojibwa Tribe."

"The simple issue here, Your Honor, is that Mr. Tormudson and the State of Minnesota have challenged the authority of the chief of the tribal council to act in the manner of other ordinary businessmen. Mr. Tormudson and the State contend that the tribe is under some special regulatory restraint not placed upon others in the business community."

"On behalf of the Respondent," continued Errol, "we will offer into evidence the Treaty of La Pointe and show to the Court that, for over one hundred years, the Ojibwa Tribe has retained the right and authority to conduct its own business affairs and that the complaint made here is without merit."

Every native in the courtroom was familiar with the hundred-year-old document that most of the white population in Minnesota never heard of. They knew what Errol was talking about.

"It should be the ruling of this Court," concluded Joyce, "that the petition for Quo Warranto should be dismissed and verdict entered in favor of the Respondent, Marie Croche Saulturs."

When Errol completed his opening statement, Jan Kiel, at the end of the counsel table, rose to her feet. The State's Attorney, obviously pregnant, had compelling features - nice mouth, nice lips, strong and full, and good facial structure, almost patrician, yet open and wholesome. Her blonde hair had been teased with her fingers. She stepped before the bench.

"Your Honor, I had announced to you that the State would not make an opening statement, but after hearing the two statements that have been made to the Court regarding the issues in this proceeding, I think, on behalf of the State, there is one matter that I should call to the Court's attention concerning this proceeding that was not addressed by either Mr. Hauck or Mr. Joyce."

Judge Clemens replied, "You may proceed to make a statement on the record on behalf of the State."

Jan shifted her stance. "Your Honor, the issues here presented have an impact beyond the question of whether or not there should be another election to determine who will be the tribal chieftain or chairman of the tribal council and beyond whether or not the investment in two corporations, as made by the tribe, is proper. Our pre-trial discovery, on behalf of the State of Minnesota, has revealed that the assets of the two corporations, the hotel and the truck line, are mortgaged to financial interests on the East coast, and the terms of the indentures state that the loans can be called and immediate repayment required, if the corporate charters of either corporation is forfeited, or if the management of the tribe, with whom the loans were negotiated, are removed from office by any means other than death. The covenants in the loan documents in effect say that if the Court rules in favor of the Petitioners, then the bankers can foreclose and put the tribe in bankruptcy. It is the position of the State that the law is the law and must be enforced and that while it would be unfortunate if the Court makes a finding that will put the tribe in bankruptcy, yet the law and not economics must dictate what the Court does. I felt that since neither Mr. Joyce nor Mr. Hauck spoke to the significance of the issues, I should call it to the Court's attention."

The Assistant Attorney General sat down.

Engel leaned over and whispered into his lawyer's ear.

"Anything more before we move on?" asked the judge.

Peter rose to his feet. "Your Honor, in response to the statement made by the State's attorney, I want to advise the Court that in the event the Petitioner is successful in these proceedings, it is the intent of the members of the tribe that I represent to re-negotiate the financing documents with the banking interests in New York. While nothing official has been done in that regard and couldn't be done until we have a favorable ruling from this Court, Mr. Tormudson and those in the tribe who agree with his views feel they will be able to re-negotiate the tribe's loans, and there will be no bankruptcy."

Hauck sat down.

Judge Clemens turned to Errol, "Do you want to make any further statement on this issue raised by the State before the Court proceeds to hear the evidence?"

Joyce rose and shook his head. "No, Your Honor. It is the

Respondent's position that there is no need to even talk about re-negotiating loans or bankrupting the tribe because Marie Saulturs, in her capacity as chief of the Ojibwa Tribe and by treaty with the United States Government, had the authority to act as she did."

"All right," said Judge Clemens when Errol had taken his seat again. "The Petitioner may call his first witness."

CHAPTER EIGHTEEN

A crimson glow, the blush of the setting sun, outlined a black ribbon cloud floating over the portage trail, its dark haze extending to the tree-lined horizon like a silk scarf, like a shroud. The body before Nina and Zona lay in a grotesque sprawl. Waves of grayness passed over the two Indian girls.

Nina, as tears of reality welled in her eyes, dropped to her knees overcome by brooding hurt. She rocked on her heels into a squatting position and with a sob began to croon the Ojibwa death song. Zona also squatted beside the body and in numb silence stared and tried to swallow the sour swelling in her throat. The enormity of the crime that had occurred took hold of her mind. Despite a rush of bitter remembrance, her lips began to mouth the ancient words of consolation;

words which are always sung in the paternal lodge of the Ojibwa dead. Her lips felt cold as she repeated the incantation.

"My father, my father, my old Wabasha?
Why hast thou left me to pine?
Why art thou gone so soon to the land of the shades?
Oh! Why hasn't thou let me, aged man, go with thee?"

The Indian girls forgot their father's drunken scenes; painful times which, at that moment, remained unspoken and hidden in their memories. They forgot the shock of the frightening encounter in their mother's bloody kitchen and forgot the missing dog that Zona bitterly accused their father of killing. Those things no longer mattered.

In the devouring gulf of their despair, the old Indian had ceased to be Yellow Fox, ceased to be the specter they had encountered in the portage clearing. He was Wabasha, the Plains Ojibwa from the land of the Saskatchewan River, the father that they did not really know, the one for whom mourning words must be uttered, the man who was the husband of their mother.

Above the roar of the cascades, the woods echoed their supplication, their adjuration that their father's spirit be permitted to cross the great river of the west and into the paradise that lay on the other side. Marie Saulturs had reared her daughters to be members of the Christian faith, but she had also reared them as Ojibwa.

When the two women finished the rite, Zona, a heaviness in her chest like a millstone, reached over and put her hand on her sister's knee. "Come," she said, "it is getting dark. We must build a scaffold." Nina, her emotion spent, feeling a sodden dullness, rose to her feet. After hesitating to look again at the broken body, she turned and followed her sister.

They climbed to the foot path and followed its muddy track until, at the edge of the portage trail, Zona pointed. She had scanned the stand of trees and selected one with branches low and strong, sturdy enough to withstand the winds and attack by prowling animals.

A harrowing headache pounded Nina's forehead. Neither spoke. Zona watched her sister with a kind of sardonic weariness. The ache Zona felt was different. Nina, she knew, hurt for a love she had lost. Zona's hurt was because of an inner loneliness that remained with her, for what might have been if Anton had been the kind of father that Zona had envisioned since she was a little girl. For an hour the two, in silence, selected and wove saplings to provide a base for a scaffold; a platform strong enough to support the body of the old Indian. The two women peeled long strips of bark for their ties. They secured the stand above the ground in the twin forks of the selected tree and overlaid the base with dry, flat slabs of bark pried from dead falls that lay on the ground. Other slabs and flat rocks were set aside to use as a covering for the body after it was lifted onto the scaffold.

In another time, the two women would have left the body uncovered for birds to pick the bones clean and would have returned after a year to place its remains in a sack for burial. But this was not the time of their grandfathers, and the two sought only to perform a death ritual that would preserve the body from four-legged animals and birds of prey until it could be retrieved for burial in the reservation cemetery.

The women removed their jackets and took off their shirts. They tore the shirts into narrow strips of cloth. Nina shrugged out of her cotton undershirt as well and bound it around the old Indian's head. Zona used her undershirt to tear into more strips. The twins ignored the mosquitoes attracted to the warmth and scent of their half-naked bodies and struggled back into their jackets.

Zona straightened the corpse and laid a long pole along the length of the dead man. Then carefully, the two began to wrap the strips of cloth around the body and the pole. When they ran out of torn cloth, they stripped off other parts of their clothing - their socks, their belts, all of their undergarments - until finally, looking down at the mummified form tied to the thick limb, they each stood barefoot in their boots covered only by denim trousers and jackets.

The women grasped the ends of the bough, lifted and struggled back up the slippery moss covered rocks and through the mud to the grove of trees where they had constructed the scaffold. With effort they shelved the body, still tied to the pole, onto the wooden platform. Without taking time to rest from their exertions, the two women placed slabs of bark and rock on the form so that it and the pole to which it was bound were completely covered. Beneath the bark on the scaffold, the girls placed the man's broken gun. At the foot of the coffin they arranged the metal traps and all of the articles that were with the man in death, except the yellow fox fur.

Zona watched as Nina squatted on the ground and dipped her palm in black mud. She smeared a line across each cheek, then loosened the lace from one of her boots and wound the strip around her arm. She reached up and separated a strand of her locks. Zona knew her sister broke off the ends to symbolically cut off her hair.

Her sister performed the ancient Ojibwa rite. Her grief expressing an infinitely, sorrowful spirit. In another century, each woman would have painted the whole of her face raven black, thought Zona, and lay aside their silver armlets and tied blackened strips of leather around their arms and neck. They would have cut off all of their hair and chanted the death song to assuage their grief. But, thought Zona, this is another time. She did not blacken her face, hers was a different kind of grief, but she did not fault Nina for having done so.

Zona sat across from her twin. All through the night the two girls remained cross-legged beneath the platform, the yellow fox fur on the ground between them. As sorrowing mothers and daughters had done for centuries, the two Ojibwa women repeated a song of death and grief in honor of the father that they never really knew.

Animals in the forest and birds listened as the wailing rose and curled until replaced by sobs and silence. The grieving lasted throughout the night. The forest creatures, sensing the nearness of death, made no sound.

Miles to the west, at abandoned Fort Charlotte, the end of the Grand Portage, where the lakes leading to the interior of the North American continent begin, the killer, Axel Denek, lay in the dark shivering, lost, and fearful of the night animals that he could hear, but not see.

Fatigue seeped through Axel's body. Sleeplessness ragged at his mind and twisted his thoughts into grotesque shapes. Time melted away, flowed back and forth, and compressed and warped the present into a maze of passages and dark tunnels. It was only an illusion borne of weariness. Axel's mind played tricks on him and bent time in a circle. Axel followed one of the maze's eerie corridors; one leading backward to the past. His mind, in a dream, laid him on the hard concrete sidewalk, where he huddled inside a cardboard furniture box, seventeen hundred miles from Boys Town in St. James, Missouri, the only real home he ever thought he had. The place his parents abandoned him, alongside Missouri's Interstate Highway 44.

At thirteen, Axel had run off and found a different kind of life on the streets of East Covina, California. Axel's mind twisted him from boy to man and into boy again. His body lay shaking, frightened, sometimes on hard concrete and sometimes on sandy, smooth volcanic rock. Axel, the man, lay on the hard surface at abandoned Fort Charlotte. Axel, the boy, felt beneath his cardboard box the uneven cracks and broken bricks of the city's dark alleyway.

Fearful of the predators, he gripped the handle of the knife and dropped into fitful sleep. Sometimes the knife he held was that which he had taken from the body of Yellow Fox, and sometimes it was another kind of knife, a sharp steak knife found in the garbage bin behind the restaurant next to the dumpster where someone had piled the furniture store's cardboard boxes. As Axel lay with his dreams and black memories, his body jerked, and he again sensed the hand that reached in and felt about in his cardboard box. The hand that slipped along his backside and down inside his pants. He felt the predator's excitement, as the hand moved inside the band of his underwear. Axel thought that if he lay very still, the animal would go away, but the hand touched and stroked the smoothness of his hairless body. The night wind in the pines above old Fort Charlotte moaned in the darkness and made a sound like sighing automobile tires rolling slowly down the street at the end of the alley.

Axel, petrified with fear, clutched the handle of Yellow Fox's knife like he clutched the sharp steak knife. The boy was confused and hoped that the predator would leave him alone, but the hand slid into the smooth crack of his buttocks and involuntarily Axel moved. He heard a chuckle of anticipation. Axel could almost feel the man's thoughts. In the night on the rock ledge at Grand Portage, Axel Denek again turned as if to offer himself in surrender to the touch of his predator. Then, lashing out, Axel drove the knife into the man's chest. It buried to the hilt, and the boy felt warm blood spread like syrup between his fingers. The blade glided between the derelict's ribs and drove death home to his heart.

At age thirteen Axel Denek killed his first man. As he rolled on the hard volcanic rock in the northern Minnesota forest, Axel awoke and remembered what he had learned on the streets of Covina. The only difference between predator and prey, between hunter and hunted, is the will to kill.

As he lay on the portage looking up at the black, star-studded sky, Axel Denek remembered the wet mackinaw coat that he had taken from the orphanage. He stood under a bridge in the rain until he was given a ride from the Oklahoma line to Tulsa by a lady who told him suggestive jokes, some of which he didn't understand. In Albuquerque, he remembered that he had kept his knees clamped tight together while a jolly older man, under the steering wheel of a truck, explained that some boys he gave rides to let him put his hands inside their unzipped pants while he drove. At a filling station in the dusty desert near Sells, Arizona, Axel saw another boy two years older than him go through the pockets of a drunk and make off with a handful of money. For two days they had been friends. The older boy had asked him if he had ever ejaculated. Axel didn't know what the word meant.

It seemed to the thirteen-year-old runaway that everyone that he met on his hitchhiking odyssey from St. James, Missouri to Covina, California talked about sex. They talked of wanting sex, doing sex, buying sex, trying sex, laughing at sex, and selling sex. Whether with men, women, or boys, sex was the common denominator that Axel Denek had found the length of Interstate 44.

The slobbering man in the furniture carton in the back alley of East Covina was the first person that Axel Denek ever killed. He hadn't meant for the man to die, but lying under the stars he remembered that as he tried to wash the blood off his clothes in the cold water that trickled down the center of the concrete aqueduct, he had not been sorry. It was just another of the lessons he had learned in the years he had grown up having to care for himself.

At the school in St. James, Missouri, Axel had been brilliant but a troublemaker. He amazed his teachers and classmates with his photographic memory, and he learned early to use his skill to his advantage.

It was the day after he had driven a knife between the ribs of the molesting transient that he met the Reverend and Mrs. Bernard Denek. The church couple took him into the parsonage, gave him their name, and raised him in the image of a Christian.

He attended the Berean Christian School and Bible College of East Covina, California, where he excelled and won a position as a disadvantaged candidate on the scholarship list of the University of California at Los Angles.

Axel Denek's education when he hitchhiked halfway across the country gave him the shrewdness to cater to the old couple who brought him to their table and were determined to save his soul. When he was in their home, he was the perfect child; the example the Reverend pointed to in his sermons. But when he roamed the streets of sprawling Los Angles, Axel developed other sharp skills, which made him a match for any that he encountered. He had learned the difference between predator and prey.

The only really good thing, Axel remembered having happened to him, was his marriage, and that, like everything else in his life, was tainted. But he had known that his wife was an addict when they married. As he shifted on the rock and tried to again sleep, Axel knew it was the sort of thing that he expected life to deal him.

Warm rays of the sun woke Zona and Nina. The two were not sure how long they slept. Both were cold and stiff from their vigil on the ground beneath the funeral scaffold. Zona scratched a mosquito bite on her belly. Her mouth was dry, she knew they needed to find drinking water. Nina rolled to her knees, also scratching insect bites.

The corpse on the scaffold had remained covered by the slabs of bark, held by flat stones, despite a wind that had come in the night bringing with it eerie treetop sounds.

"Axel did this," Zona finally accused. "He's the only one who could have."

Nina looked at her sister. "You don't know that. There can be others on the trail besides us."

"Don't you see the paddles?" asked Zona, exasperated with her sister. "Those are the paddles that made the markings along the trail when we were following Axel's track's. He's dropped them."

Nina shook her head. "Zona, we don't know that those are the same paddles. It may have been somebody else's tracks that you and I followed."

Zona looked at her sister in disbelief. "You still think that he loves you, don't you? Even after he was willing to let someone cut your finger off, you still think he loves you. I had enough of Axel Denek when I found out he was married. I don't know how you can think you're in love with a married man."

"Do you think he is married now?" asked Nina dully. There was mystery in her question. Since Duluth, she couldn't get over the obsessive sense of everything going wrong.

"Isn't he?" inquired her puzzled sister.

Nina shrugged.

Zona missed the hesitation; the fleeting look of apprehension that crossed her sister's face. "You're still in love with him, aren't you?" she repeated.

Nina nodded. She looked up at her sister, a plea in her eyes. "Axel could not have done this," she said again.

"Shit!" said Zona. "Let's go find him."

"How?" asked Nina.

Zona pointed. There's only one set of tracks leading in here and leading out of here. Whoever is leaving those tracks is the one who killed Yellow Fox."

"Whoever it is will be dangerous," whispered Nina.

"So are we," said the twin resolutely. With that she stepped off on the trail and Nina followed. It did not occur to either girl to fear the man they set out to track. They were Ojibwa and vengeance is an ancient form of Ojibwa justice.

CHAPTER NINETEEN

Tom Boushey started his climb to cross the Grand Portage at the National Park Service's restored stockade. Voyageur games and historical displays were featured events at the gathering down below. The sounds of the celebration floated up to the Indian. At first the pathway was uphill and rocky. Behind the climber, the sun formed big smooth diamonds on the surface of Lake Superior where breezes picked up dark purple water and spit out whitecaps. Boushey saw that the boots of many hikers had stomped the trail bare. The sound of automobile traffic on Highway 61 at the start was muffled by the trees and thick brush that lined the trail, but eventually the sounds of civilization disappeared altogether leaving only nature's muted stir of insects and birds.

The Indian balanced a pack on his shoulders. Sweat already

stained the cotton shirt beneath its padded straps. He brought no camping equipment, only a blanket, some food, fishing gear, and a knife. Head down and with long strides, the Ojibwa read the signs in the pathway before him. The trail worked its way through thick woods, over numerous deadfalls, into muddy depressions, and up and down ridges. Heat, black flies, and mosquitoes added to the Indian's discomfort. At first the trail was beaten hard and wide by tourists who tramped into the interior far enough to tell that they had once walked the great carrying place. Beyond the sound of highway noises, the trail narrowed.

There were fewer footprints, and the tracks followed a rock ridge leading the Indian away from the great lake. The stands of trees lining the portage thickened, but there were also meadows of grass that concealed curious eyes of wildlife who, interrupted in their feeding, watched his passing. Tom Boushey carefully looked for any sign that a canoe party had left the trail and stepped off into the woods.

Mike DuLac, a native park ranger, had told Tom that two young girls and a man were seen carrying a canoe on the portage the day before. The ranger had not talked to the canoe party and had no idea where they were headed. But from DuLac's description, Tom was certain that the women in the party were Nina and Zona.

At half trot the Indian put behind him the first miles of the portage which led upward on dry ground. He tried to make as much speed as he could in the first part of his morning journey while he was fresh from his night's sleep and because he knew that the muddy track below the beaver pond would slow his stride.

The warming sun had driven away the rising mist and fog when the Ojibwa schoolteacher topped a ridge and saw spread below him a sheet of water that blocked the muddy trail.

Nina watched as Zona grabbed a handhold on a root and pulled herself to the top of the slab of granite that barred their way. In their creation the portage's rock outcropping was formed of mixed pink molten lava with a dash of black and folded together like a marbled cake. About them were many variations of this theme creating brilliant colors and beautiful forms. "Do you see the tracks?" called Nina.

"Yes. He didn't try to go around. He climbed up here where I am."

Zona worked her way along the narrow ledge above the cracks in the rocky earth that spilled out bubbling white rivers of crashing water and plunged into the canyon below. The fresh scraping of lectin on the face of the stone showed her where their quarry had climbed. "This way," she waved to her sister.

Nina grasped the root and began the tortuous climb to the top. As she followed Zona, her mind again wandered back to their father.

Nina remembered vividly the bloody encounter she and her sister had with their father in their mother's kitchen on the day their father left. "It is strange how fast our emotions change when we are eight years old," she thought. The night before the encounter she had felt love and sorrow. That was the night when both she and Anton Saulturs had spied upon her mother through the window. Nina hadn't meant to spy. She didn't think her father intended to either.

While playing their game, Nina had silently ran to the back of the cabin to hide from her sister. She had been surprised to see the figure in the shadow of the trees. Anton was so engrossed that he didn't know Nina had entered the yard behind him. The curious eight-year-old watched her father's motionless form.

In their chasing game, Nina had chosen the edge of the old icehouse for her place to hide. Zona was nowhere to be seen, still searching for Nina along the lakeshore on the other side of the cabin. Nina remained very still. She couldn't make out what had fixed her father's attention. The twin grasped the side of the icehouse slat fence and slowly climbed to get an unobstructed view.

The attention of the man in the shadows continued to be intently focused.

Silently Nina pulled herself to a height where she could look beyond her father's head. The driveway through the woods to their home was long, and at its end approached the house from the backside. The front of the unpainted cabin faced on a high bluff overlooking the lake. The dwelling was small and open, filled with dark wood and glass. In the window of their home, she saw the reason that her father stood transfixed.

Beyond the glass was the reflection of two figures. They were outlined by the flames dancing in the stone fireplace. There were no other lights.

Nina stood on her toes on the slat and peered through the darkness. She saw the man in the kitchen offer her mother what appeared to be perfectly clear crystal. As he did so, he laughed and brushed back hair that fell on his forehead. On the kitchen table she saw there was cheese. Her mother sliced the cheese and then accepted the drink. The man turned his face to the light, and in a flash Nina recognized him, their schoolteacher, Tom Boushey.

The young girl realized that Anton was looking through the window at her mother's friend. Both watched from the darkness as Tom reached up and stroked her mother's hair. His face in the dancing firelight appeared to be drinking her in. The night was surprisingly warm. Her mother placed a piece of the cheese in Tom's mouth and again they laughed. Marie then took the schoolteacher's arm and walked out of the light.

Nina peered down at Anton. The shoulders of the man drooped as he turned from the empty window and with long strides set out across the back yard. She remembered that she had seen a vulnerable man walk into the woods. Even at eight years, the girl knew Anton was reacting to a betrayal, like the time when Nina had skipped school to stay all day in the Grand

Portage museum, and Zona told their mother. Nina wasn't sure of the reason, but she recalled that she had wanted to run after her father, to take hold of him, gather him in, convince him that she shared his sadness. Anton disappeared into the trees. Nina remembered that she had remained standing unseen on the fence, looking back at the empty window. Some of what she had seen she understood, and some she did not. She liked her mother's friend, their schoolteacher, Tom Boushey, but she loved her father, Anton Saulturs.

Nina climbed down from the slat fence and circled the house, overwhelmed by sadness. A light was turned on. It summoned her from the inside, but she didn't go in.

The front door of the house opened, and a shaft of brilliance cast out on the ground. A masculine form was framed in the doorway. Giant shadows inside the house danced on the walls and ceiling. In the dimness Nina saw the silhouette of the schoolteacher as he reached out with his strong hand, touched her mother's arm, then stepped out into the night.

For a long moment her mother stood in the doorway, then the woman had called, "Zona, Nina it's time to come in."

As Nina slowly walked towards the open door, she remembered her mother had only called for the twins, she had not called for their father, Anton Saulturs.

Above her, from the ledge, Zona shouted her name.

"Nina!" Her sister's voice shook the girl from her reverie. She grasped the root that stuck out from a crevice in the rock and hauled herself up onto the ledge. "I'm right behind you," answered Nina. She put aside her childhood memories and scrambled after her sister.

Engel Tormudson opened the door and stood aside while Marie Saulturs stepped out into the parking lot. The many faces in the hallway of the courthouse watched the two contestants go out the door together.

During the afternoon recess, Peter Hauck had approached Errol Joyce's counsel table and said abruptly, "My client would like to talk alone with your client, do you have any objections?"

Peter spoke to Errol Joyce without looking at Marie Saulturs.

Errol turned to his client. "Do you want to talk to Engel?"

Marie cocked her head and looked up at Peter. "What does Engel want to talk about?" she asked.

Peter replied, "Engel would like to have one last opportunity to talk with you about settlement of this case before either he or you are required to take the witness stand. I told him that it didn't make any difference to me if it wouldn't make any difference to Errol and if it was agreeable to you. So, I'm just asking."

Marie pursed her lips and looked back at Errol. "I don't have any problem with talking with Engel."

Errol lifted his hands. "O.K., Peter and I will go tell the judge that the recess will take a little longer than we thought, and you two talk. You might get something worked out."

Peter said, "Engel is downstairs in the corridor on the first floor. There is such a crowd in the courthouse, he's asked that I see if you will meet him down there so the two of you can go out in the parking lot where you can have some privacy."

Marie had left the two lawyers who were headed for the judge's chambers and met Engel at the back door of the courthouse. He had without a word opened the door, and the two walked out into the parking lot and away from the crowded courthouse. A breeze stirred the leaves of the aspens that lined the parking lot. As they walked in silence, Marie wearily looked up at the ramparts of the Sawtooth Range, and for a fleeting instant wondered where her daughters were.

At the end of the parking lot, Engel Tormudson leaned against the back of an empty pick up truck with his arms folded. Marie faced him.

"You wanted to talk to me?" she asked.

Engel nodded. "I was relieved," he said, "to hear from the County Prosecuting Attorney that the dead girl down at the college was not your daughter."

"Thank you," said Marie.

Engel seemed to search for words to get started. "Whether you believe it or not," he said, "I don't want anything unpleasant to happen to you or your family."

Marie was puzzled by the man's opening. She guessed that he was referring to the unfortunate events that had occurred in her daughters' dormitory in Cloquet. So Marie again said, "Thank you," and waited.

The man started again. "I feel very strongly, Marie, that the way you are going about running the business affairs of the tribe is wrong."

"I gathered that," said the woman coldly. "You said as much in the lawsuit you filed."

"I have always considered you to be my friend, Marie, ever since we were kids on the reservation."

The woman waited for him to continue. "If it involved anything else, I wouldn't say or do anything that would interfere with that friendship. But, friends or not, when it comes to tribal affairs, I think I must do whatever is necessary for the good of the tribe."

Marie was still at a loss as to what the man was driving at. "I assumed that," she said, "when you filed this lawsuit, but I don't agree with you."

"Will you agree to resign as chairman of the tribal counsel? Stay on as chief of the tribe, but resign so we can elect a new chairman of the tribal counsel, if I dismiss this lawsuit?"

Marie shook her head. "Being chief of the tribe is only a ceremonial position, Engel, you know that. It's the chairman of the tribal council that runs the business affairs."

"It might save a lot of embarrassment," warned Engel.

"Engel," said Marie Saulturs. "I don't care if I am the chief and chairman of the tribal council. I really don't. But I do care that our people do the things they have to do to provide jobs for Ojibwas. As long as I am chairman, I intend to operate Wedgewood-Ben and the hotel corporation. If I resign as chairman, you would get elected, and you have already said that you would sell off the truck line and undo all the things the tribal council has done this past year to make jobs for our people."

"It just makes good business sense, Marie," argued Engel. "You've gotten the tribe so far in debt that we're going to lose everything." The cadaverous Indian waved his arms. "Ninety cents out of each dollar you take in now goes back east to pay the debt service on the loans. Your plan to bring casino gambling and high stakes bingo to the reservation under the new gaming law depends on bringing crowds up here to the North Shore that we are never going to have."

"How do you know that unless we try it?" asked Marie.

Engel turned as if to walk away, then turned and looked back at her. "You're going to have to bring three thousand people a week into the hotel to make any casino operation profitable. We don't get that many in the height of the tourist season around here, much less during the other nine months of the year."

"You said the Wedgewood-Ben Truck Line and the hotel wouldn't work either," reminded Marie, "but they did."

"But only to the extent that it sends money back to New York to pay the bankers," said Tormudson heatedly.

"And also pay a payroll to about ninety of our people," responded Marie.

Engel's hands sliced through the air. Looking back toward the courthouse, Marie could see members of their tribe were looking out the doors and windows watching their every move and gesture. "There is no use arguing again about that," said Engel. "That's not why I asked to talk with you."

"Well," said Marie, "why did you ask to talk with me? You knew when I contested your lawsuit, I wasn't going to resign."

Tormudson paused as if again gathering his thoughts. "I told you that I was your friend, Marie, and I wanted to do nothing to harm you or your family, and I meant that. But if you force me to do it, I will make it so embarrassing for you that you will be forced to resign your office."

Marie's eyes narrowed as she tried to read the man's mind. "What do you mean embarrass me and my family?"

Engel nodded his head sharply. "Exactly that, Marie."

"And what is it that you propose to do to embarrass me into resigning my office?"

The man looked around the parking lot. He wanted for no one but Marie to hear his words. "Do you know where Anton went the day that he left you?" asked the Indian.

At the mention of her husband's name, Marie stiffened. Almost twelve years had passed since the bloody affair in their kitchen and Anton had stepped out of her life. Marie's face did not betray her surprise at the mention of her husband's name. "No," she said coldly, "I have no idea where Anton went."

Then she asked, "Do you?"

Engel nodded. "Yes, I do."

Marie waited, because she knew that whatever was in the plan that Engel had to get her removed as chairman of the tribal council, a part of it had to do with Anton.

"Your husband drove that old car of yours across the border at the Pigeon River Bridge and stopped at the first bar on the Canadian side of the border. I was there," he said. "He came in mad, and he got roaring drunk. I was the only one there that he knew, and he spent about three hours talking my leg off before he went out and got in your car and headed on north into Ontario."

Engel paused to see what kind of impression his words were having on Marie, but her face was impassive. "He told me about pulling your daughter, Nina, out of the bay before he left." Engel looked at Marie, but her face didn't change expression. "He told me that you were pregnant, and carrying his baby."

Marie nodded. "My third daughter," she said. "Anton has

never seen his daughter." Marie's statement was almost a challenge.

Engel continued with his story. "Anton told me about the time that he was teaching at the university in Chicago, a short course on Native Americans, and how when you arrived on the campus you and he hooked up together and married. He told me how he had wanted to go back to the woods. He didn't like Chicago, didn't like teaching, didn't like people, and didn't like crowds. But because of you, he stayed and put you through the university to get your degrees."

Marie looked at Engel. Her face was as hard as stone. She remembered the times at the university when Anton would do his heavy drinking in the evening and announce that he was going to leave her and leave the city so he could go back to his lakes and woods and live with the animals that he loved. And she remembered how Anton would sober up in the mornings and reluctantly return to his job at the Indian Culture Center on the university campus. Anton, Marie remembered, was twenty years older than she. She didn't think that it was so much that he loved her as it was that he felt an obligation to take care of her, like she was his child. It was only in the evenings in Chicago when he drank heavily that he became ugly and abusive.

Marie looked at the man leaning against the pickup truck.

Engel was studying her as he prepared to say his next words.

"Anton," he said ominously, "also told me before he left about Zona and Nina."

Marie stiffened, and her thoughts again drifted back to the traumatic last encounter that Anton had with the twins.

"Is that all?" asked Marie coldly.

Engel nodded without speaking. He had said all that he thought he needed to say.

"I love our tribe, as much as you do," said the woman. " I have to also do what I think is good for the tribe, and right now I think that is to keep you from becoming chairman of the tribal council."

Marie turned on her heels and started walking back across the parking lot to the courthouse. "Think about your family," called Engel.

Marie heard his words, but she continued walking straight ahead. She felt a sob choke in her throat. She knew what Engel Tormudson meant, and her thoughts did turn to her family.

Judge Dorothy Clemens laid her robe across the back of her chair and poured cups of coffee for Jan Kiel and herself from a pot sitting on a warmer behind her desk. Both Peter and Errol declined her offer.

"I'm sorry your clients couldn't settle their differences," said the judge.

Jan Kiel stood by the office window and nursed her cup of coffee.

"If what Jan has said is right," said the judge, "my ruling will make the difference between whether the tribe goes bankrupt and scatters or stays solvent."

"Not necessarily," said Peter. "My people are certain that they can get any necessary refinancing."

Errol didn't argue the point. He reserved his arguments until the court was in session where it counted, when the statements and evidence went on the transcript of record. He knew Dorothy Clemens well enough that any discussions in chambers were off the record and would not determine her course of action.

Jan Kiel spoke up. "We've got two stubborn people here. Both of them are trying to do what they think is best for the Ojibwa Tribe, but because of their stubbornness, they are going to destroy the tribe."

Judge Clemens said, "When we go back into the courtroom, after we complete the examination of Doctor Zahn, I'm going to recess this case overnight, and we will start back again at eight-thirty tomorrow morning. This will give your clients a chance to have some second thoughts. Do you have any objection to that, Peter?"

The lawyer shook his head no.

"Jan, Errol?"

Both of the other lawyers shook their heads. "All right," said the judge. "That is the way we will proceed. Maybe both of you ought to explain to your clients that a lean settlement is worth more than a fat lawsuit when you've got a lot at risk."

CHAPTER TWENTY

Ivella Zahn sat on the raised witness chair beside the judge's bench and patiently waited as the procedural confusion revolved around her.

Peter Hauck was on his feet angrily voicing his objection to Errol Joyce's cross-examination of the witness. Peter insisted that it is the duty of the judge to rule that Minnesota courts had jurisdiction, and consequently the witness could not be cross-examined on her knowledge of the government files concerning the one-hundred-year-old Treaty of La Pointe.

Errol Joyce was standing beside Hauck at the judge's bench insisting that he was entitled to cross-examine the witness concerning the Treaty of La Pointe before the judge ruled on the jurisdiction issue.

"State's rights," insisted Peter Hauck, interrupting Joyce.

Errol Joyce leaned across the bench and stabbed his finger at the yellow tablet upon which the judge had been making her notes.

As Ivella sat on the witness stand beside the quarreling lawyers, she tuned them out of her mind. She thought in amusement to herself, "How many times over the years have I been on the witness stand or gone before legislative committees and ad hoc groups and heard the interested parties try to limit my statements, my points of view, my philosophy." Some did it by disruption in schoolhouse auditoriums. Some did it by parliamentary technicality, and some did it as Peter was attempting to do in the courtroom, by objection.

Dorothy Clemens leaned back in her high back chair, and with arms folded, let the two lawyers argue while she made up her mind as to whether or not she would rule as Peter was suggesting, that as a matter of law, her court had jurisdiction to remove the chief of the tribe from her office, or whether as Errol Joyce argued, that she should reserve her ruling until the conclusion of the examination of the Government's witness as to the extent and enforceability of the treaty that the government had made with the Indian tribe.

The witness calmly sat with her hands folded in her lap and looked out across the room full of faces that were focused on the bench.

Alejandro was seated beside Terry Whitehall-Banning. His jaw was set and his swarthy face and mustache projected the grim feeling that had settled over him when the judge first indicated that she would reserve her ruling on the jurisdictional issue and permit Errol Joyce to cross-examine the Government's witness about the files that revealed the history of the Treaty of La Pointe. The government lawyer clutched his briefcase in his lap.

Ivella saw Terry look down at the briefcase with amusement.

Both Peter Tormudson and Marie Saulturs, from their chairs at the two counsel tables, were watching and listening intently in an effort to catch the words of their lawyers. The fat, balding court reporter, seated near the witness, was pounding his stenotype machine furiously as he watched the lips of the contesting lawyers.

Ivella noticed that Jan Kiel sat back in her chair at the counsel table and did not indicate any bias as to the outcome of the argument. Her pad was lying on her lap, where she idly tapped it with the end of her pencil and waited.

Beyond the rail, the benches were completely full, and the eyes of the spectators were closely following the proceeding taking place at the judge's bench. Spectators lined the wall and stood in front of the windows. The courtroom was full and overflowed through the open door into the hallway.

Finally Judge Clemens' voice sharply interrupted the lawyers. "I've heard enough," she said. "I think you can take your seats."

Errol Joyce ended his rebuttal in mid-sentence. With Peter Hauck, he returned to the well of the courtroom and sat down.

Ivella saw Engel whisper into Peter Hauck's ear and Peter shake his head. She turned to look at the judge on the bench beside the witness box. Dorothy Clemens had turned back to her yellow note pad and was filling it with penciled lines, but the witness could not decipher what she was writing. Finally, Judge Clemens raised her head.

Leaning toward the court reporter, she read her ruling. "The court will take the objection of the Petitioner and the Petitioner's request for Summary Judgment on the issue of jurisdiction under advisement." With her pencil, the judge made a correction on her tablet and continued reading. "The Court is of the opinion that before the Court can rule on the Petitioner's request it must afford the Respondent the opportunity to present its evidence as to whether or not the Treaty of La Pointe must be taken into consideration by the Court in arriving at its decision." Peter Hauck started to get to his feet and protest, but Judge Clemens raised her hand. "Let the record show that the Petitioner takes exception to the Court's ruling, that the ruling will stand, and, Mr. Joyce, you may proceed with the cross-examination of the witness."

Peter sat down and started writing. Errol picked up his pad and walked over to the empty jury box, where he could position himself to watch the witness and also the judge's reaction to the witness's answers to his questions. The State's lawyer and Peter turned their tablets to a fresh page and waited for Joyce to begin his cross-examination.

Ivella looked out at the bench where Alejandro was seated. Their eyes met for a moment before she turned to the task before her. The woman knew that her answers to the lawyer's questions would be the answers of the United States Government on whose behalf she had been subpoenaed to testify. Her role was not to offer up, by her answers, her own personal views and biases. She was pragmatic. It is the position of the Government that she must present in her answers.

"Doctor Zahn," started the lawyer standing at the jury box, "before Mr. Hauck made his objections, you had testified that you were asked by your superiors to review the Government's files concerning the Treaty of La Pointe, and that you did so before coming here to testify. Isn't that correct?"

"It is," replied the witness.

"Did you review all of the Government's files concerning the treaties the Government made with the Northern Ojibwa band of the Chippewa Nation?" asked the lawyer.

"I reviewed all of the files I could find," she replied.

"In your opinion, were any of the files missing?"

"I have no way of knowing," said the witness. "I asked that the storage archives in Maryland deliver to my office all of the files, and I assume that they did. I have no reason to believe otherwise."

"In your review of the files, did there appear to be any gaps or anything missing that would indicate to your mind that there might be a file on this subject that you have not seen?" asked Joyce.

"Again, I have no reason to believe anything was missing," answered Ivella.

"You were satisfied then," asked Joyce, "that you have reviewed all of the correspondence, memoranda, research papers, and reports of conversations concerning the Indian treaty?"

"Yes," replied the witness, "and also the files concerning the draft form of documents including the final executed document."

"Doctor Zahn, how many different treaties did the United States Government make with the Chippewa Nation?" asked the lawyer.

"Objection!" Peter Hauck was on his feet. "I object to the testimony of the witness concerning any other treaties for the reason that it would be immaterial."

Joyce spoke to the judge. "I'm laying a foundation, Your Honor, concerning the 1854 treaty."

"Overruled," said Judge Clemens.

Peter returned to his seat.

"Did you understand the question?" asked Errol.

The witness answered, "Yes. There were five."

"Based upon your review of the Government's files, did you reach a conclusion as to whether or not either of the parties had broken those treaties?"

Ivella stared out past the audience as she framed her answer. To herself she thought bitterly, " I want to say 'yes - the Government has broken every treaty it ever made with a North American tribe.'" But aloud she said, "Mr. Joyce, the Government files in substance recite that the treaty that was made was not working as the parties intended and consequently a subsequent treaty was made to which the Indian tribe and the United States Government was a party."

Peter Hauck arose to his feet again. "Your Honor, I should like at this time to object to the hearsay testimony. The Government's files themselves are the best evidence."

Errol looked over at the judge. "This is cross-examination. On direct examination, this witness testified that she had examined the Government's files. Mr. Hauck has presented this witness as an expert on the matter of the Government's treaties with the Ojibwa Tribe. Consequently, even if the testimony is hearsay, Mr. Hauck has waived his client's right to object."

"I'm going to overrule the objection," said Judge Clemens. "The Petitioner did present this witness on direct examination as its expert and was qualified by reviewing the Government files. So, I will rule that the Petitioner has waived its right to object on the grounds that the files would be the best evidence, or on the grounds of hearsay. You may proceed."

Errol looked at his notes. "Dr. Zahn, I have forgotten where I was, so at the risk of repeating myself, would you please tell me whether or not your review of the Government's files indicated that either the Government or the tribe failed to carry out their part of the terms of the treaty?"

"My answer," reminded the witness, "was that the files indicated that there was a succession of treaties between the United States and the Chippewa Nation, and each of these were characterized in the Government's files as not working, and each of the treaties was a substitute."

"You found nothing in the files to indicate that the Government had broken the treaties with the Chippewa Nation?" asked Joyce.

"I did not find any statement in any of the files," replied the witness, "in which the Government, or any government official, admitted that the United States broke the treaty."

"In any event, the tribes, by these treaties, contracted to give up a substantial portion of land in exchange for the Government's promises. Isn't that correct?"

"Yes," replied the witness. "Substantially all of what is the upper portion of the State of Wisconsin and Michigan and all of Minnesota north of Lake Superior and to the west to the Dakotas was land which the United States recognized that the Indians owned and controlled and was giving up in exchange for the promises in the treaty."

"Do the Government's files show whether or not any of that

land was returned to the Ojibwa Tribes?"

"No," the witness replied. "None of the lands were ever returned to the Chippewa Nation, although there were some lands up by Grand Portage, Nett Lake, and Fond Du Lac, which were retained by the Ojibwa Tribe as reservation lands."

Errol Joyce watched the witness closely as she gave her careful answers to his questions. Her answers were honest but were the most favorable response she could give on behalf of the United States Government to each of his questions.

"Doctor Zahn, in your examination of the files, did you find from your review of any of the documents that the Chippewa Nation ever gave up its right of self-government and self-determination in the conduct of its affairs?" asked Errol.

Doctor Zahn looked out at the front bench where Alejandro was watching her intently. The witness was not intimidated by the government lawyer's presence in the courtroom, but she was aware that her representation on the witness stand was for the United States. By her answers, she was determined to fairly present the Government's position, not because the government attorney was present, but because Ivella felt strongly her duty.

But she was determined also not to color the truth.

"My review of the Government's files and the treaties," said the witness, turning again to Errol Joyce, "is that there was no bargaining between the United States and the tribe concerning the right of the tribe to conduct its own affairs internally on the several reservation lands that were preserved by the tribe and recognized by the United States Government. So my answer to your question is no. There is nothing in the files or treaties that limit the powers of the tribe to conduct their affairs."

"Let me present to you a hypothetical question," said Joyce. "Assuming that before the Treaty of 1854, or for that matter the treaties that preceded that one, the Ojibwa Tribe had the right and authority to choose its own chieftain and chairman of its tribal council. In your opinion, did the tribe retain that authority and right after the execution of the treaty, or did they surrender that right in the contract that was made?"

"In my opinion," said the witness, "that authority and right was retained by the Ojibwa Tribe and was not contracted away to the United States Government."

Errol continued. "Based upon your examination of the files and the treaties, did you find anything to indicate that the tribe surrendered to the United States its right to conduct its business affairs in any way that it saw fit?"

"I did not," replied the witness.

"Would you agree then," asked the lawyer, "that, following the Treaty of 1854 and until today, the Ojibwa Tribe has had the authority to create business corporations and to transfer its funds in and out of those business corporations or between those business corporations in such manner as in its opinion was to its best interest?"

Ivella Zahn thought very carefully about the question put to her by the lawyer. She looked down at Alejandro. She saw the intense concentration in his eyes, and she knew what he was thinking about; the relationship of the State of Minnesota to the two corporations that were being investigated. Very carefully the witness answered again. "My answer to your question is, yes, except insofar as the State of Minnesota has retained the right of control over the corporations."

Joyce asked, "You're referring to the hotel corporation and the Wedgewood-Ben trucking corporation which are organized under Minnesota law?"

"Yes," replied the witness.

"And you're stating that you don't give an opinion, one way or the other, as to the effect that organizing Minnesota corporations as vehicles to operate those two businesses has upon the authority of the tribe to function in the State of Minnesota?"

"Yes," replied the witness.

"And that is because you don't know, or you don't have an opinion?" asked Joyce.

"I have an opinion," said Ivella after a long moment.

Errol raised his eyebrows. "What is that opinion?"

"Objection!" said Peter Hauck.

"Overruled," said the judge. "This is cross-examination."

Ivella Zahn shrugged and looked out at Alejandro Doman. "I believe that the tribe, if it forms and uses a Minnesota corporation to conduct its business, is subject to the laws of the State like any other business venture."

"No more or no less restrictive?" asked Joyce.

"Yes," nodded Ivella Zahn. "In my opinion, no more or no less restrictive."

"So if a businessman could transfer his funds into a business corporation that he owns and controls, you think the tribe could do the same under the treaties, is that correct?" asked the lawyer.

"Objection!" said Peter Hauck. "That goes to the ultimate issue before this Court, the propriety of transferring the funds."

"Sustained," ruled Judge Clemens.

Marie Saulturs stirred in her seat at the counsel table.

Ivella Zahn's straight testimony, she thought, gave her a chance to win. There was a stoic look on the faces of Peter Hauck and Engel Tormudson, seated at the other table, staring at the witness. Out in the courtroom, on the first bench beside Terry Whitehall-Banning, Alejandro Doman pursed his lips and exhaled slowly. His section head was not going to like what was being said here, he thought.

CHAPTER TWENTY-ONE

During the court recess, Errol Joyce and P.M. Gregory stood in the hallway and watched the confrontation between the deputy from the Bureau of Indian Affairs and Alejandro Doman, the government lawyer who made an unexpected appearance during the morning session.

"What are you doing here?" asked the woman.

Alejandro walked with her to an open hallway window. The two stood where Errol and P.M. could observe their animated conversation. "I do what I'm told, Ivella, just like you," defended Alejandro.

"What kind of report did you give the Solicitor General to make him want to spend his department's travel dollars on a trip for you to Minnesota?" asked the woman sarcastically.

"He wants me to merely observe," replied Alejandro lamely.

"Observe me, or observe the trial?" The woman spoke sharply.

"Both," admitted the lawyer.

Ivella raised her arms in disgust and walked away. She followed a knot of women down the stairs. Alejandro watched her turn on the stair, his swarthy features set in deep thought. He felt as if there had been set off a sudden declaration of war between them.

Ivella Zahn stood beside one of the columns on the front steps of the courthouse. She continued to seethe with anger. The woman could not suppress her resentment to Alejandro's spying presence. Doctor Zahn was so preoccupied with her anger that it was several moments before she realized that there was another person standing on the opposite side of the column. The woman was startled to see Terry Whitehall-Banning staring at her.

"Hello," said Terry. Her smile was engaging and innocent. The girl's teeth were perfect and she was exquisite in a childlike way.

Doctor Zahn nodded. "Hello," she replied dryly.

"We were sitting on the same bench up in the courtroom," said Terry.

"Yes," replied Ivella.

Doctor Zahn could see that the young woman was caught up in an excitement and exuded a demeanor that seemed to almost rush out of her, like a child who has burst through the kitchen door to tell some great secret that only she knew. Ivella, for the moment, forgot Alejandro's presence as the other woman stepped to her and held out her hand.

"My name is Terry," she said. "Terry Whitehall-Banning." Her smile was almost embarrassed. "Whitehall was my mother's maiden name, and Banning was my father's name. They're divorced," she said.

Ivella took the girl's small hand in hers and felt herself gripped tightly as if the young woman was reluctant to pull away from her.

"I am Ivella Zahn," she replied.

"Yes, I know," said Terry, "I heard your name when you were introduced to my boyfriend."

Ivella's eyebrows raised.

Terry stammered. "Peter Hauck, the lawyer, when you were introduced to him," she explained. "That is when I heard your name."

"You say he is your boyfriend?"

"Sort of," grinned Terry. "I'm his personal secretary. He is married now to my aunt, but they're going to get a divorce," she said.

A puzzled look came over Ivella's face.

Terry's eyes suddenly showed a hint of fear, and the smile fell from her face. "I shouldn't have said that. I shouldn't have told you that."

For reasons that Ivella couldn't understand, the girl standing before her appeared a reflection of herself. Ivella could almost feel her loneliness, and it reminded Ivella of her young years back in the boroughs of New York. But the reasons for her feelings were beyond Ivella's understanding. The girl standing before her was absolutely beautiful. She appeared to be everything that Ivella was not, when she was a plain child growing up in New York City.

Terry looked away. "I'm always doing something like this," she said. "I don't know why. Sometimes I just talk to strangers." She looked back at Doctor Zahn. With a wry smile she said, "It's probably because I didn't have anyone else to talk to. My mother and father were divorced after I was born. I was raised by my aunt. That's why I use both of my parents' names," she confessed. "They didn't come around very much when I was growing up, so I kept them around by using both of their names." She laughed. "You think that's silly, don't you?"

Ivella shook her head.

To herself, Ivella thought, "This is a strange conversation."

Terry's face tightened and she was silent for a moment while she considered whether she should say anything more to the lady that stood on the courthouse steps. She looked up at Ivella and blurted out, "I'm going to have a baby."

Doctor Zahn was stunned by the girl's unabashed announcement. The woman stammered, "Congratulations." Ivella could think of no other reply to the startling disclosure.

Terry dropped her eyes and looked down at her feet, then looked back at the other woman. She said, "I just had to tell somebody. I just had to tell somebody," she repeated again. "Peter is my baby's father," she said in a soft whisper and looked closely at Ivella to see her reaction.

Ivella stared at the girl without replying. She understood how Terry could blurt her news to a perfect stranger. Ivella had that same need to talk to, and confide in, someone when she, herself, was growing into young womanhood. Ivella had experienced the temptation to stop perfect strangers on the street and pour out her heart to them because she had no mother who would listen to her and no father that she could turn to.

Doctor Zahn reached over and took the girl's hand between hers and held it. "I hope," said Ivella, "that you will be very happy."

A look of gratitude came over Terry's face. "You mean that?" she asked.

Ivella nodded. "Yes, I hope you will be very happy," she repeated.

Terry looked into the older woman's eyes. "You don't think I'm crazy for telling you when I don't even know you?"

"No," said Ivella. "I don't think you are crazy for telling me."

"I just had to tell somebody," whispered Terry.

"I understand," said Ivella.

Terry threw back her head and said, "It's so wonderful. We had three glorious days camping up on the lakes. I haven't been to see a doctor yet," she explained with a shrug. She shyly withdrew her hand "But I know I'm going to have Peter's baby. It's going to be a beautiful baby."

Ivella nodded. "I'm sure it will."

A startled, expectant look came over Terry's face as she looked across Ivella's shoulder. Doctor Zahn turned and saw the lawyer, Peter Hauck, standing in the doorway signaling.

"I've got to go," said Terry. She leaned over and kissed Ivella on the cheek. "Thank you," she whispered, and turned and ran toward the door.

Doctor Zahn watched the young girl put her arm around the lawyer's waist and walk with him into the courthouse. A twinge of sadness touched her heart. It was as if she had heard Terry Whitehall-Banning's story before.

CHAPTER TWENTY-TWO

The young Ojibwa, Billy Gendron, wore denim trousers tucked into leather boots. The Indian unzipped the fly on his new jeans, and with effort reached inside to pull at his cotton underwear. After a fumbling delay, Billy wrapped his fist around himself, and, with a feeling of relief, let loose his water against the back of the porcelain fixture.

The stiffness of the pants, worn for the first time, and the tight metal zipper irritated Billy the same way it had when he relieved himself at the back of his cabin in the morning mist.

"I hate to break in a new pair of jeans," he grunted to the man standing in the stained urinal beside him. In the men's room on the bottom floor of the Cook County Courthouse, the two Indians relieved themselves and stared at the dirty wall opposite their noses.

"Our economy is in a fuckin' mess no matter what those lawyers upstairs say," Billy grumbled. "There is no demand for lumber. The steel mills have stopped shipping taconite. Silver Bay is now a ghost town. Commercial fishing disappeared when Lake Bass left Superior. Half the grain elevators in Thunder Bay and Duluth are empty. There are no jobs for Indians or anyone else."

Billy appeared strong and tall, a man in his late twenties at the peak of his physical vigor. His wide shape filled the entire urinal stall. His fat face was almost perfectly round, with a ruddy complexion framed by black hair.

The old Indian in the other stall was gray haired, bent, and took longer to empty his bladder than his younger companion.

"It's old age," Moses, the elder with a biblical name, felt compelled to explain.

By the window at the end of the row of urinals, wooden partitions boxed in toilet stools, one of which was occupied and had its door closed.

The younger shook himself, zipped his front, and stepped back to wait for Moses to finish.

"I went down to Silver Bay to see if I could get a job in the mines back on the Iron Range. They weren't hiring," Billy continued. "Then, I went over to Superior on the Wisconsin side, and I stood in line for three hours with about a hundred other people, all of us trying to get one of the five jobs they had on the sluice line in the paper mill. I didn't even get off the sidewalk, inside the building before they announced the jobs were filled." Billy frowned, "Then I went to the State Unemployment Office over in Duluth. All they had available was a night job cleaning offices and washing windows at three dollars and fifty cents an hour. How the hell can I live in Duluth on three dollars and fifty cents an hour," asked the Indian, "and have any money to send to my family to eat on?"

"No way," agreed Moses.

"If I didn't have kids that I want to have it better than me and my woman had - if it was just me and her alone - I'd take off in the woods and live off the land. I'd fish, trap, and say to hell with the government bait." Billy shrugged. "But if you love your family," he said, "you can't do that."

"Nope," agreed Moses, "all you can do is keep looking for that job, tell your family to tighten their belts, and go up to the agency office and get your handout of government bait."

The old Indian finished at his stall and shuffled over to the sink to wash his hands.

"I got a cousin," said Billy, stepping out of the old man's way, "who lives over on the Canadian side. He gets thirteen thousand a year and doesn't have to pay taxes on any of the food he buys as long as he stays on the reservation."

Moses dried his hands. "Just government bait, only more of it," he said dryly.

"Well," said the younger Indian, "my cousin over there in Ontario can't find a job either. Fact of the matter is he says that unemployment in his province is greater than it is in Minnesota. It's just not fair. It's just not right," Billy spoke vehemently. "In countries as rich as Canada and the United States, a man ought to be entitled to at least have a job so he can give his family a decent living." He added, "It's not fair to say we should be satisfied to sit on the reservation and take the handout of the government bait."

Old Moses grunted and pointed a bony finger to the ceiling. "That's what the trial upstairs is all about. I voted for Marie Saulturs, and I'm going to stand by her through this whole thing, no matter what. She did right by the tribe when she built the hotel and bought that truck line."

"Yes, but you've got a daughter that got one of the jobs," said Billy. "I didn't get no job. It makes a difference who the companies help. If they don't help you get a job and make wages, it don't mean nothing to you."

The old man shook his head. "Before Marie organized those two companies, there weren't no jobs for any of us up here. Do you think Engel Tormudson would have done any better if he had been sitting in Marie Saulturs' chair?"

"I don't know," admitted the younger Indian. "But I do know I haven't made a decent day's wages since I last worked as a guide up on the Gunflint Trail. Seasonal work with the tourists helps some, but a man can't get through the winter and feed his family decently without a steady job."

"Why don't you get behind Marie then," asked Moses, "instead of just complaining like Engel Tormudson is doing upstairs? At least Marie's trying."

"Engel says all the cash the companies are taking in is being sent back east to pay off the mortgage money that the tribe borrowed, and we ain't keeping any of it here."

"But," argued the older Indian, "Marie's now going to get casino gambling in the hotel under the new law that the Government passed last year. That'll add some more jobs."

"Engel says we won't have big enough crowds up here on the North Shore to make any money off of a gambling operation."

"Well what are you going to do?" asked the old man. The planes of his face were angular. His dark, hawkish features seemed never to have known a smile. "Engel isn't going to get us any more jobs. He wants to sell off the Wedgewood-Ben Truck Line. We will lose all the truck jobs if he has his way. He hasn't got any plan."

"I got four kids," explained Billy, talking with wide sweeps of his arm. "I'd like for them to grow up on the reservation. I don't want them to leave the North Shore so the only ones left are old folks who will die out. But my kids won't stay up here like I did, to work all their lives and wind up without enough to support a family."

Billy patted his shirt in an absent searching gesture. "How in the hell can we make the bunch in Washington know that Ojibwas don't want charity, we just want jobs."

The older Indian had no answer.

When Billy and Moses went out the men's room door, the closed portal on the partition that shielded the toilet stools swung open and its unseen occupant stepped out.

Alejandro Doman, the Washington, D.C. lawyer, had sat on the toilet and heard everything that was said. Even the last words the young Indian uttered as he stepped out into the hall.

"Goddamn government bait!" The declaration echoed around the room.

CHAPTER TWENTY-THREE

Zona reached back and grasped Nina's hand. She helped her sister scramble to the top of the massive rock out cropping that overhung the plunging river. A spray of refreshing air was chan neled up through the rock openings and gave the girls relief from the heavy dank atmosphere that the afternoon sun had pressed down on the portage.

Zona unbuttoned her jacket. The coarse cloth chafed her body. Without socks, the boots had rubbed a blister on one of her heels. Nina also complained of the chafing. In the cool updraft, Zona let her half-naked body feel the soothing moist air. She was tempted to stand naked at the edge of the ledge. After closing her eyes and taking deep breaths, she turned to her sister sitting on the ledge beside her. "Why don't you take off your jacket?" she invited.

Nina secretly admired her sister's curves that shaped her figure and made everyone aware that the two were not identical twins. Nina's own figure was well proportioned, but slim and flat. Zona undid her belt and slid her pants down to her knees. As she prepared to kick off her boots and stand naked in the cool air, a deep male voice startled the girls. "You sure look good from here!"

Nina turned, startled. Zona grabbed at her pants and pulled them over her hips. Standing behind them on the ledge, between them and the portage pathway, was the grinning figure of Axel Denek.

Somewhere on the trail, Axel had left his suit coat and tie. His trousers were rolled half way up his legs, and from his shoes to his ankles his feet were caked with mud. He had buttoned the cuffs and collar on his white shirt to ward off the insects. His face was shadowed with a day's growth of beard.

Zona saw a glint of lust in his eyes. "Pervert," she thought as she zipped her pants and buttoned her jacket.

While dressing, Zona took a quick note of their position of disadvantage. She and her sister were on the ledge above the cascades; a place from which there was no retreat. The rock bridge over which they had come to reach the ledge lay between them and the portage trail, and Axel stood on it with his feet spread and his hands on his hips. Thrust in the man's waistband at his side, was a hunting knife.

Nina scrambled to her feet. "Axel!" she cried, "You're safe!" She ran to him.

Zona yelled, "Nina, no!"

But she was too late. Her sister had reached the man and he had his arm around her waist holding her to him.

Nina clasped her arms around Axel's neck in happiness, and he kissed her. But as he did his eyes remained open and he never took them off of Zona.

"You son-of-a-bitch," said Zona.

Axel grinned. "I always spoke well of you, Zona," he said.

Nina clung to her man and looked across the ledge at her

sister. "Zona, what a horrible thing to say," accused Nina.

Zona's eyes narrowed as she looked at her sister. "The knife, Nina. Look at the knife!"

At Zona's words, Axel Denek's hand moved to the hunting knife at his waist as if to cover it.

Nina drew back and looked down. "Where did you find that?" she breathed. Her eyes searched Axel's face.

Across the ledge, Zona answered her bitterly, "He didn't find it, he took it." Axel Denek continued to hold Nina about the waist and finger the handle of the blade. The afternoon sun glittered on the silver sunburst design that Yellow Fox had worked into its handle. There was no mistaking its owner. Nina and Zona knew that it was the same knife that Yellow Fox laid on the log beside their spread fingers.

"Where did you find that?" Nina spoke again, almost in a whisper.

"I found it on the trail," said Axel Denek. His eyes stared across the space into the eyes of Zona Saulturs, and he knew that she knew that he was lying.

Nina, with her hand still on Axel's shoulder, turned to her sister. "He found it on the trail," she repeated.

"He's a lying son-of-a-bitch," said Zona grimly.

Axel's arm that encircled Nina's waist tightened, and he looked down at Nina. With a half whisper he said, "The scorn of a jealous woman." And then he laughed.

Nina lifted her chin. Axel was right, she thought. Zona was still jealous that Axel had chosen Nina rather than her sister.

"What did you do with the canoe?" asked Axel trying not to make his inquiry sound too anxious.

"We hid it," began Nina.

Zona interrupted her. "Nina, no. Don't tell him were the canoe is."

Nina was brought up abruptly by the look in the face of her sister. Something about Zona's stance and look put her on guard. Nina turned to peer up at the face of the man who was holding her. The look on Axel's face was one the girl had never seen before - bitter, hard, and almost savage; a look of pure hatred. The man squeezed her with his arm that was wrapped around her waist, and his hand continued to grip the hilt of Yellow Fox's hunting knife.

"Where did you hide the canoe?" Axel spoke out of the corner of his mouth while watching to see if Zona made any move to get off the ledge.

"Back down the trail," stammered Nina. She looked at her sister with a glint of guilt in her eyes.

"Where down the trail?" asked Axel.

"I'm not sure exactly," said Nina. She was confused by her sister's message that was being sent to her by the hard look in Zona's eyes.

Axel drew Nina to him. "Not so tight!" she exclaimed.

"Where down the trail?" repeated Axel.

"I don't know exactly," stammered Nina.

"Then show me," said the man.

"No!" said Zona. "Nina, don't show him where the canoe is. He just wants to get the canoe to get across the border and to get away."

Axel Denek's features softened. He took his hand off the knife, and taking hold of each of Nina's shoulders he turned her to him. "Nina," he said, "don't let your sister's jealously ruin our plans. I hid the formula in the canoe. I know where the paddles are. Let's go on to Lavel University as we planned. After we get there we will get married, and Zona can pick up that old Indian's traps and broken gun and go on back down to Grand Portage and say whatever she wants to about us."

Axel slipped his arms around Nina, pulled her to him, and kissed her fully on the lips. A long shuddering kiss that caused Nina to close her eyes almost, but not quite, in surrender. Two words spoken by Axel filtered through her mind: "broken gun."

CHAPTER TWENTY-FOUR

The courthouse parking lot was empty. The pickup trucks, including those that had parked on the lawn, were gone, for members of the Ojibwa band that occupied the hallways and chambers of the county building did not remain to engage in small talk or review the day's happenings. They vacated the town and scattered up the North Shore like a flock of Canadian geese preparing to settle in for the night. The sun dropped behind the mountains, and the sky over the fishing village started its early evening coloring.

Engel Tormudson and his lawyer, Peter Hauck, sat in the empty jury room on the third floor of the courthouse. The lawyer had sent his young woman friend over to the Harbor Inn and escorted his client into the chambers reserved for jury deliberations so the two could talk in private about their evidence.

"Our problem," said Peter, "is to convince the judge that Marie Saulturs' intention when she transferred the tribal funds over to the two domestic corporations was to act contrary to the wishes of the tribe, thereby acting outside the definition and authorization contained in the Treaty of La Pointe. The treaty," Peter explained, "requires the chief to act with the consent and in the interest of the tribe as a whole."

Peter pointed his finger at Engel. "Errol Joyce has got probably thirty members of the Ojibwa band sitting out in that courtroom who probably will defend Marie's actions." He continued, "If they support their chief, then legally that is all she has to prove. The fact that there are an equal number of tribesmen who are prepared to support your view to the contrary is not enough to justify the Court in issuing the Quo Warranto order."

The lawyer got out of his chair and walked over to the window to look out at the waters of the harbor, which had begun to pick up the coloring from the sky.

"You've got a popular chief sitting out there in the courtroom," said Peter, "and if the tribesmen continue to support her, we're going to lose this lawsuit."

"And if they don't support her?" asked Engel.

"Then I think you've got a chance to win." Peter turned back to his client. "Unless you know some way to discredit that woman, you're going to find that she's wrapped herself in a cloak of integrity that the judge is going to accept. On this issue the burden of proof is on us, and if the Court is in doubt as to who wins, then things will remain as they are."

"Marie Saulturs can lose that support pretty fast," said Engel quietly.

"How so?" asked Peter.

Engel Tormudson thought for a moment, then pulled his chair up to the long table. "Sit down," he motioned.

The lawyer took his seat again. Engel leaned across the table and in a low voice asked, "Do you know why Marie Saulturs always wears gloves?"

"I hadn't thought about it," shrugged Peter. "A fancy dresser, I suppose," he replied.

Engel shook his head. "Nope. She wears gloves to hide the fact that one of her fingers is missing."

Peter stared across at the Indian, puzzled. "She's lost a finger?"

Engel nodded.

"How did that happen?" asked the lawyer.

"She cut it off," said Engel.

"She what?" Peter was startled by the response.

"She cut off her own finger," said Tormudson.

"Why would she do that?"

"It's a family matter," said Tormudson. "She did it to conceal the fact that she has violated an ancient tribal taboo, and if the other members of our tribe ever knew what I know, then she would not have the support that you tell me that you're afraid of."

"What is this secret that you know?" asked Peter Hauck. "And why the hell would anybody purposely cut off his finger?"

"She did it because she thought she was ransoming her own children, the twins, Nina and Zona Saulturs."

"That's preposterous!" exclaimed Peter.

Engel nodded. "It's true," he said. "She did it because she thought that she would lose her children if the twins ever found out that Anton Saulturs was not really their father and that their father was their mother's own first cousin, Tom Boushey."

"How do you know that?" asked the lawyer.

"I just know," said Tormudson. "When Marie went down to the university in Chicago, she was pregnant with the children of Tom Boushey. She never told Tom, and as far as I know, to this day, Tom doesn't realize that he is the father of the twins. While Marie was at the university, she met an instructor that was some twenty years older than she was, Anton Saulturs. Anton was from Saskatchewan, and he was an instructor on the faculty in the Native Americans' Program that the university had at that time. Tom and Marie had just gotten back from the protest marches on the Mandan Reservation. While they were in the Dakotas, Tom didn't know it, but he had gotten Marie pregnant. Marie went off to the university, hooked up with Anton, and he agreed to let Marie name him as the children's father, and they married. Anton loved the woman."

"How did you find that out?" repeated Hauck.

Engel shrugged again. "Anton got drunk and told me. He said Marie was still in love with Tom. He and Marie tried to make a go of their marriage. She did have one kid that was his, the youngest, but the other two are Tom's kids."

"It gives me no joy to tell you this story," said Engel. He looked directly at this lawyer. "I think I was in love with her myself, once," he added softly. "I have to admit she's an unusual woman." Tormudson sat back in his chair and continued. "Things had been going badly for Anton in his marriage. Marie told Anton that she didn't love him and wanted him to leave and let her have custody of the children. Anton got mad, he was probably drunk, and he threatened to tell everybody that the twins were Tom Boushey's daughters. The tribe knows Tom and Marie are first cousins. Everybody knows the Anishinibe taboo. According to Anton, Marie accused him of holding her daughters hostage by threatening to expose their secret. Anton made some stupid remark to the effect that if Marie thought that, then she should buy them back by paying the Sioux ransom. He didn't mean it. It was the liquor that was talking, but before he could stop her, Marie picked up a knife and severed her ring finger at its second joint. It was a bloody mess, according to Anton. She offered him the finger in payment for her children. Anton got sick. He threw up all over their kitchen. The twins came in looking for their little dog. Anton screamed for them to get out. It was a bad scene."

Engel concluded, "Anton said he got in the car and was across the border at the Pigeon River before he found the kids' little dog asleep in the back seat. Anton went native after that and took to the woods. He always was peculiar."

"That's a hell of a story," said Peter.

Engel nodded. "Yes. And if the other members of the tribe knew Marie violated the Chippewa taboo by having children by her first cousin, Tom Boushey, and then tried to hide the truth by paying the Sioux ransom, she wouldn't be chief any more. She would be shunned. Our people feel strongly about these things. Marie knows that. That is why she always wears gloves. She doesn't want to talk about her missing finger. She's afraid of making a slip, and the truth will come out."

"We're not going to use that story in the courtroom," said Peter Hauck.

Engel looked at him darkly, "We will if we have to, to win."

"If we did, we would ruin the life of not only Marie but of her daughters as well," said Peter. "From everything I've heard, those two children have turned out to be bright, perfectly normal children, even if their parents were first cousins."

Tormudson nodded. "Yeah, they apparently got all the good genes, but they are still children of a forbidden relationship. The tribe will never forgive their mother."

"How about the lives of the twins?" asked Peter. "Will the tribe ever forgive them?"

Engel shook his head. "That can't be helped."

"Is it so important," asked Peter, "that you be chief, rather than Marie, that you would ruin the lives of three of your own tribe?"

Tormudson nodded. "Yes. The whole of the tribe is more important than any member of the tribe. I'm sorry if it affects the girls, but they will move away from the reservation and their lives will go on. As you said, they are bright kids, but I've got the rest of the tribe that I've got to worry about. That's why I hired you as my attorney. When we go back into the courtroom tomorrow, I expect you to put Marie on the witness stand and ask her to remove her gloves."

"You play hard ball," said Peter.

"That's right," said Tormudson. "When necessary, I play hard ball."

CHAPTER TWENTY-FIVE

Marie Saulturs sat in Errol Joyce's office staring out of the large picture window that overlooked the harbor. Boats across the bay rose and fell in the gentle swelling that rolled in from the lake. The sunset burnished the seawall and lighthouse with a golden glow.

The lawyer and his client had been discussing Engel Tormudson's offer made in the courthouse parking lot. Errol Joyce was appalled by the woman's description of her marriage to Anton and their separation.

"You're not going to let Tormudson blackmail you into quitting, are you?" Joyce couldn't believe the woman's suggestion.

"Despite what I told Engel, I can't fight him on this," said Marie levelly. Errol sat at his desk and looked across at the woman who continued to watch the restless waters in the harbor.

"You're not the first woman who got pregnant by a man other than her husband," he said gently.

Marie turned and gave him a faint smile. "That's not the point," she said. "It was forbidden for Tom and me to have children."

"You have two very bright, perfectly normal girls," said Joyce. "How can anyone in the tribe fault you? What happened occurred almost twenty years ago. These are different times. People have different attitudes."

"Errol," Marie shook her head sadly, "after all these years, you still don't understand my people. It is an ancient Anishinibe tradition that first cousins, like brothers and sisters, may not have children. It is taboo, forbidden, a sacred ban of our tribe."

She leaned toward the desk and looked at him. "When I realized that I was pregnant and that Tom was the father, I was so frightened. I feared my baby would be deformed, or have some mental defect, or even be a Mongoloid baby. There is every good sense in the world for the Anishinibe taboo. I was afraid, and I was sorry for what we had done." Marie bit her lip. "And I thanked God when my daughters were born whole and normal. But still I know Tom and I took a risk that we should never subject a newborn life to."

"But all that is past now," said Joyce.

"Not for my people, it isn't," said the woman.

Marie laughed a sarcastic sound. "Ojibwas are just as bigoted as any other people. We have our rednecks, our hypocrites, and our narrow minds, just as you do. When the tribe learns what Tom and I have done, we will be outcasts. Engel will tell them, and we will be outcasts."

"We will win this lawsuit," predicted Joyce.

"If we do, then what?" asked Marie.

"Legally you will remain in charge of the business affairs of the tribe and do the things you plan to do to help your people these next five years."

"They would never let me help them. My daughters and I would be shunned. How could I do anything for the band under those circumstances?"

"If Engel gets in control and starts selling off assets, the tribe is certain to go bankrupt and scatter," said Joyce quietly.

"And if I get a favorable decision out of Judge Clemens and try to stay on, the tribe will also go bankrupt, and we will scatter."

Errol Joyce stood and walked to the sliding glass door that opened his office onto the balcony that stuck out over the waters of the harbor. He stood in the doorway and breathed in the sea air. "Then the band will be broken up," he said. "In five years there won't even be a Northern Chippewa Tribe, except in name," he added.

"Some will go to other reservations up in Canada or down in Michigan. Or," she smiled wryly, "become integrated into American society and go to the cities to live on welfare."

"Engel thinks he's right," mused Errol.

Marie nodded.

"And you think you're right," said the lawyer.

Again Marie nodded.

"And the tribe suffers," the man concluded.

"The tribe suffers because of Tom and me, but I can't do anything about it now, except take my daughters and leave."

"If they will even go with you," reminded Joyce. "What is going to be the reaction of Nina, Zona, and your youngest girl when they are told?" he asked.

"I don't know," whispered the Indian mother.

CHAPTER TWENTY-SIX

After the court recessed, the two officials from Washington, D.C. delayed their walk to the Harbor Inn. Instead they watched the lake change its colors as the sun went down behind the trees on the skyline behind them.

Ivella Zahn and Alejandro Doman sat on the top step in front of the Cook County Courthouse and looked down on the town of Grand Marais. The harbor below spread out to the breakwater and into the endless lake beyond. Ivella indicated, for the Washington lawyer, the location of Artist Point, the lighthouse, and the Coast Guard station. The blue waters extended to the horizon. The smudge of an ore boat making its way from west to east was the only blemish on the vista below.

Ivella had changed into corduroy slacks that she wore on her field trips. Although her destination was the circuit courtroom in Grand Marais, in Washington she had packed for the trip as if she were going again to one of the reservations. Alejandro was still dressed in his business suit, white shirt and tie, the uniform of eastern lawyers. A frown wrinkled Alejandro's forehead as he sat beside Ivella. She thought that there was a strange, nervous unease about the man. At first they talked and digested the evidence they heard in the courtroom. In his cross-examination of witnesses, Errol Joyce repeatedly turned everyone's attention to the disconsolate state of the economy in northern Minnesota. Before the recess, the lawyer had held in his hand sheets of numbers from the Bureau of Labor Statistics that confounded Peter Hauck's witnesses who sought to expound only on jurisdictional issues. The Grand Marais lawyer, who represented Marie Saulturs, by his cross-examinations, was broadening the scope of the inquiry despite objections of his opposing counsel. Through it all, Alejandro thought, Engel Tormudson, seated beside his counsel inside the rail, exhibited a tenseness that revealed an apprehension.

"You did a good job on the witness stand," admitted Alejandro. "The Solicitor probably isn't going to like Judge Clemens' decision, but you fairly stated the Government's position."

"If Joyce had asked me if the Government screwed the tribe when it wrote those treaties, I would have said 'yes'."

"Well, I'm glad the judge didn't let him ask you that question," laughed Alejandro.

Ivella wrapped her arms around her knees and said, "We've got to figure out some way within the federal regulations to keep this band from going bankrupt."

The lawyer sitting beside her didn't reply to her suggestion.

"It's a funny thing," mused Alejandro. "If you sit in the courtroom, close your eyes, and just listen to the words, all of the problems the Ojibwas have up here in the Arrowhead Country are the same problems that my father deals with for the Union everyday back in Jersey."

A look of amusement came over Ivella Zahn's face. She drew her lips into a tight smile. Her young lawyer friend from Washington was speaking of the non-existent jobs that her Indians had sought for years.

Alejandro wrapped his arm round his knee and leaned back on the concrete step. "I don't know if I ever told you," he said to Ivella, "but my father for thirty years has been a business agent for the Teamsters Local back home. When I was growing up I used to go with him to deliver bags of food to union members who were out of work. I remember one Thanksgiving we made forty-two stops in South New Brunswick. Gus had to borrow a truck, we had so many bags to haul. And do you know what?" he continued.

Ivella asked, "What?"

Alejandro put his tongue in his cheek and looked back at the waters in the harbor below. "The look in the eyes of those people Gus and I delivered the groceries to back in Jersey was just the same as the look in the eyes of the Indians that were talking to you upstairs in the courtroom."

Ivella smiled. "Is that right?"

"Yes," he nodded. "It's not so much a look of despair or a look of defeat but rather a look of bewilderment, as if they don't understand why there are no jobs." Alejandro did not repeat to Ivella the conversation he had overheard in the men's room. "Up in Jersey where my father works, the men wanted to feed their families, but they had no money, and they resented the bags of groceries the Union gave them."

Ivella nodded, "I know what you mean," she said. "I've seen it before."

Alejandro pulled hair across his bald spot. "You know, if my father were here, he would organize this tribe into a union. If he were here, I think he would try to get the tribe to appoint a business agent, shop steward, and go out to the employers on the North Shore and make them give the tribe jobs at a decent wage."

Ivella laughed. "That's easier said than done."

"Well," nodded Alejandro, "if Little Gus was here, he would try it."

"Who would he name as business agent," asked Ivella, "Engel Tormudson, or Marie Saulturs?"

"Oh," said Alejandro, "from what I've heard, I imagine Gus, for the short term, would like to have Engel Tormudson as the business agent. Engel seems to worry most about doing a fast fix, doing immediate things, but over the long haul I think Gus would want Marie Saulturs to head up his union. You can tell from the way that woman talks that she is planning ahead five and ten years for the tribe."

Ivella Zahn didn't respond.

"I'm surprised. I really am. I'm surprised that the Indians up here aren't all that different from the people back in Jersey." The lawyer stared off at the horizon as he spoke.

Ivella shrugged and asked, "Did you expect them to be?"

"Yes," said Alejandro turning back to her, "I really did. I don't know why, but I really did."

"You still thought of them as savages, did you?" Ivella smiled.

"No, not savages. I didn't think that. It's just that you don't think of an Indian being a mechanic, or a carpenter, or a stone mason, or a forester."

"Or," said Ivella, "an accountant, an engineer, a lawyer, a hotel clerk, or the pilot of an airplane."

"That's right," said Alejandro. "You just don't think of them in those kinds of jobs. You don't think of them like you do the labor force back in New Jersey."

"I remember one time," the man continued, "my father delivered a package of food to a kid of one of the union families. The kid threw it down on the porch at the front door. He said they didn't want no charity. He was probably just repeating what his father and mother thought, but was afraid to tell Gus. It's kind of like what the Indians were saying in the hall upstairs awhile ago when they were talking about government bait. They don't like the handout from the Government under our present tribal system any more than the kid from Jersey liked the handout from the Union. They just want a job."

Ivella nodded. "Dignity. They are just like you and me. They want the dignity of earning their own living, and they don't want to be patronized. That is what we're litigating about upstairs; Marie's plan to provide jobs for Ojibwas so they won't have to take the government bait."

"Tell you what," suggested Alejandro. "When you and I get back to Washington, why don't you come over to the house. You'll like my wife, she's a good cook, and we can go through the federal regulations and see if we can find some loopholes that will help the tribe up on the reservation."

Ivella was pleasantly surprised by the suggestion. "Let's do that," she smiled.

CHAPTER TWENTY-SEVEN

Errol Joyce stood on the wood balcony overhanging the Grand Marais harbor and watched the light of the Cessna aircraft top the seawall and the aircraft settle on its pontoons into the calm waters of the bay. The harbor lights colored it as it taxied across the water to the dock below the warehouse.

Joyce shook his head in wonder. At six o'clock that evening he had called the telephone number the Chairman gave him. Three hours later, Neville Mines, LTD delivered the accused Gary Faulks to his dock. "Jesus!" Thought the lawyer. "How much money does Neville Mines, LTD have to produce results like that?" He remembered the ultrasound image of Jan and his child that MacKenzie produced at their meeting. The company has a lot of money, Joyce surmised. For all he knew, the multi-national corporation could have bought up the entire hospital and its records. It didn't have to bribe some clerk in the business office.

Two men remained out on the lighted dock while Gary Faulks, a short fat man with quick steps, mounted the stairs and bound into Joyce's law office. As Joyce stepped from the balcony into the room, he saw through the hall door the figure of P.M. Gregory looking over Joyce's client. Joyce closed the door and indicated to the couch as the place for the new arrival to sit.

"You going to leave that open?" Faulks asked, pointing to the door to the balcony.

"Yes." Joyce took his chair behind his desk.

The man nodded his approval. "Good! I'll light up a smoke then."

Errol Joyce waited and watched the man nervously search his pockets for a cigarette and matches. After puffing his first cloud of smoke, he looked about for an ashtray. Joyce handed him one from the desk.

The two men spent a moment looking each other over as if doing a preliminary appraisal.

"Your Indian trial over?"

Joyce shook his head.

"You going to get me off when my turn comes?" asked Faulks.

"Maybe."

The man on the couch shrugged. "If you are as good as the Chairman thinks you are, I should get to go home tomorrow."

Joyce ignored the suggestion. "Where is your home?"

"Toronto. Mostly it is St. Paul, but the Chairman figures I should spend the next few months on the Canadian side until things cool down a bit."

"MacKenzie says that as chairman of Neville Mines, he had your authority to hire me to defend you. Is that so?"

"If he says so, it is."

"He says so."

"Then you are my lawyer."

"Why do you need a giant corporation to hire me? Why didn't you call me if you wanted to hire me?"

"Didn't know you."

"Why would a man like Adam MacKenzie bother with interrupting a flight from Nevada to Toronto to land his plane at Duluth to meet me?"

Faulks shrugged and stubbed out his cigarette. " Perhaps he thought he owed me."

"MacKenzie owed you, or the corporation he works for owed you?"

"Both."

"What is your connection with MacKenzie?"

"Why do you have to know that just to get the criminal arraignment set back a couple of months?"

"Mr. Faulks, I don't have to represent you, and I am not going to represent you if I don't get some straight answers about what happened down at the college."

Faulks pursed his lips and then nodded. "It's no secret. I was with Canadian special services attached to the Chairman's command when he was on the general staff in Korea. He offered me a job when I got out to work for him."

"Doing what?"

Faulks sat on the edge of the couch and raised his finger. "I do whatever the Chairman pays me to do. Special stuff he is bothered with."

"Like breaking into college dormitories?"

"No one can prove I broke into any college dormitory. I wasn't in the building when the campus cops stopped me."

"The State says you took a purse from the girls' dormitory with credit cards and other identification that places you in the building."

"Bullshit! You know better than that, Mr. Joyce."

Joyce waited to see if his probe took him any further.

Faulks stared back at Joyce. "The only place that the purse and credit cards place me is in the parking lot where the girl dropped them when she got in the car. I was just holding them when I got stopped right after that," he said.

"MacKenzie says you told him that the dead girl is not Zona Saulturs." Faulks nodded.

"How do you know?"

"Somebody reported finding the body of the dead woman and had to have called campus security because they came barreling down the street and went right past us when the girl dropped her purse while getting into the car."

"What girl?"

"The Indian girl; the one they said was dead."

"You saw her after the campus security were called?"

"Sure. How do you think I got her purse?"

"Do you know who the girl was?"

"Sure. Zona Saulturs. The other one was her sister Nina. They were with some guy I didn't know. They drove off in the Honda the police described."

Joyce leaned across the top of his desk. "Did you ever meet the Saulturs twins before?"

"No."

"Then how did you know the girls in the parking lot were them?"

"MacKenzie gave me pictures so I could identify them."

"If the dead woman is not Zona then who is the woman you killed?"

"Mr. Joyce, let's get something straight. I didn't kill anybody. I am a private investigator not a criminal. I am licensed by the State of Minnesota, and I have had offices in St. Paul for fifteen years now. I did investigations for MacKenzie while I was on his staff in Korea. I went to work for his company after I got out of the service and then started my own company. I have a legitimate operation. Sometimes we cut corners by putting a tap on a telephone or looking around where somebody lives when they leave the doors unlocked, but I am not a killer. I don't know who the dead woman is that they found. MacKenzie gave me photos of the Saulturs twins. I never heard of them before, but I was told their mother is chief of the tribe that runs one of the Indian casinos..."

Faulks stopped talking and put his head down as if to weigh whether he had said too much.

"Go on," Joyce said. "Attorney-client relationship bars me from revealing whatever you tell me, and if I did, it couldn't be used against you in court."

The client leaned back on the couch and started over again.

"Neville Mines wanted a book that the Chairman thought the girls had in their possession in the dormitory. MacKenzie mailed me photos of the girls so I could find out where they were living on campus without having to make any inquiry to the college staff. That was easy enough to do. I probably could have found their room without their pictures. I was on campus that night because I was searching their room to find the book the Chairman was after."

"You broke into the dormitory room?"

"I am not charged with breaking and entering. That is not what the arraignment is about."

"How did you get in, if you didn't break in?"

"The door was unlocked. Shit - most college dorms always are. Anyway, I searched the room and didn't find the book. When I was in the girls' room, there was nobody else in there, and there was no dead naked girl on the bed. I left the room but hung around the campus trying to figure out another angle. Several minutes later, these three, the twin girls and the guy, came out of the building arguing. They got in a car over in the parking lot and one of the girls dropped something. About that time, a campus cop came speeding down the street with its lights flashing. After it went by, the car in the parking lot pulled out and headed down the road. I went over to where the car was parked and found Zona Saulturs' purse. I took it over to the street light to see what was in it, and another campus cop came driving up and stopped me."

"You recognized Zona Saulturs from her picture?"

"It was her alright. If you get my arraignment put off until they find her, the State will have to dismiss the charge against me. That woman isn't dead."

"But another woman is dead!"

I don't know anything about that. And no one but you knows I was in that room that night, and like you say, you can't tell what I told you - attorney-client stuff. I knew that before you mentioned it. I've worked with lawyers before."

"I'll bet you have," Joyce said.

Errol rose from his desk and silently stood in front of the window. He watched lights from an ore boat low in the water, plowing its way east. He turned to the man again. "What was the book that Neville Mines wanted so badly from the Saulturs girls?"

"A diary."

"A diary one of the girls was keeping?" asked the puzzled lawyer.

Gary Faulks rose and stood beside Joyce at the window. They looked down at the dock where the aircraft was parked and the two Neville pilots waited. Faulks looked out the window as he spoke quietly. "Mr. Joyce, I am not going to take a fall for the Chairman of Neville Mines, LTD, or anybody else. I told MacKenzie that, if I had to, I would take the witness stand and testify at my arraignment to get off. And I told him if I did I would tell the truth why I was there and how it was that I knew the Saulturs girl was not dead. I picked up her purse in the parking lot, and no one can prove otherwise, and finding a purse is not a crime. You and MacKenzie are the only two that know I actually got into the room. MacKenzie doesn't dare incriminate himself by saying he knew I was in the room, and you can't because of the confidential relationship between attorney and client. I told MacKenzie that he either fixes it so the arraignment is put off until the Saulturs girl shows up again, or I tell it all."

"Look Faulks, if what you say is true, then whether you testify or not, you probably will get off on the murder charge, but what makes you think MacKenzie won't be so mad that he will see to it that you get stuck with the breaking and entering charge? He will just deny that he put you up to it. You're probably on the company's payroll for other work you have done for them, so the fact that he hired you wouldn't necessarily make him an accomplice. Men in his position don't get their hands in the dirty stuff like getting photographs of the girls for you. It looks like you have an out for the murder charge, but just because I can't say anything because I am your lawyer won't get you off on the breaking and entering charge if MacKenzie takes after your ass."

Faulks shook his head. "You are forgetting the book."

"You said you didn't find the girl's diary."

"Look Mr. Joyce. Here is what Neville Mines and the Chairman don't want known. The diary he sent me after did not belong to either of the girls. It was their mother's diary."

"Marie's?"

Faulks nodded. "It was very simple. The Chairman learned that a diary was kept by the chief of the Grand Portage band."

"Marie Saulturs."

"Yes. And for some reason, the Chairman thought one of her daughters had it. And in the diary, in her own handwriting, the woman wrote about a scandal that would have had her thrown out of the tribe. If that happened, then a guy by the name of Engel Tormudson would become the new chief, and he don't want no casino."

"You are talking about the Grand Portage Casino or the Fond Du Luth Casino?"

"Both."

"The Chairman thought that if he could come up with a way that would get rid of the woman, then the new chief would get the tribe out of the trucking business and casino business by defaulting on the loans. Neville Mines would then offer to buy up the gaming licenses and land title in the bankruptcy proceedings and let it be run by a board of Native Americans that could qualify to hold the license, but who would be controlled by the Chairman."

"Can you prove that?"

"You bet I can. Down in St. Paul I have a computer full of

files that would convict MacKenzie and his man Omer Wallace of fraud if they don't get me out of this."

"That's why Neville Mines is paying my fee," said Joyce.

"You got it friend," Faulks said smartly.

"Tell you what!" Joyce replied. He returned to his desk and spun around to the keyboard of his computer. "I am going to give you a better deal. Do you want a better deal?"

"Sure."

"Ok. First, you're going to give me a written statement of everything that has happened. Everything, including how MacKenzie and his company attempted to get around the ownership requirement of the Indian Gaming Act and control the casinos. Second, you are going to waive your right to make me keep quiet about the confidential conversations we have had so I can make a trade with the State. I will tell the State that Zona Saulturs is not dead in exchange for the State's agreement not to prosecute you for breaking and entering the college dormitory. Oh--Shit!"

"What?. . ."

"Jan knows," Joyce said, lowering his forehead to the keyboard. "The State's lawyers already know they have filed a faulty charge against you!"

"Why do you say that?"

Joyce sat up again in the chair. "I just remembered, Marie Saulturs called me yesterday afternoon and said the police know both of her daughters are alive. They even asked her if she knew where the girls were."

"So?"

"If the police know the dead woman is not Zona Saulturs, then we can be damn sure Jan Kiel and the prosecuting attorney know that also. The State is keeping the charge against you open until the last minute when they will have to dismiss it, so as to get Marie's daughters to come out of hiding."

"Why didn't they tell me?" asked Faulks.

"You were found at the scene with the contents of Zona's Purse. They think you are guilty of something. You are not going to get any sympathy from Jan or the prosecuting attorney." Errol Joyce turned back to the keyboard. "If I don't have anything to trade, I will claim the door was unlocked and you took nothing; that it was all just a stupid mistake. You will give me a floppy disk containing all the files you have on MacKenzie in your computer down at your St. Paul office. Also, you will give me permission to show your statement to MacKenzie to make sure Neville Mines doesn't make any more runs at trying to take over the Indian casinos and make sure that son-of-a-bitch MacKenzie gets out of the lives of Jan Kiel and me forever. You agreeable to that?"

Faulks nodded. "I guess, but what about the dead woman? What if they want to charge me with the death of the woman they did find?"

"They are going to start the murder investigation all over again when they find the identity of the dead woman. If you had nothing to do with her death, you don't have anything to worry about. But, that's your problem. And if they do charge you for that murder, you go find yourself another lawyer."

Joyce waited. "You going to do it?" he asked.

Faulks rose and walked to the window again. He looked down at the Neville Mines' aircraft rocking in the bay.

"Yes," he said softly.

CHAPTER TWENTY-EIGHT

In the evening dusk, Zona sat across the small campfire and watched its light flicker across the two faces opposite her. Axel had his arm around Nina, who lay her head on his shoulder. Zona wondered if the flickering points of light that shown in her sister's eyes were signaling second thoughts about the intentions of the man who held her.

"You tell him, Zona," whispered Nina.

Axel's arm tightened in irritation. "Why can't you remember where it is, if you think Zona can?"

"I don't know the woods like Zona does," said Nina lamely.

Once she had tried to pull away from the man, but he continued to hold her. Axel Denek had permitted Zona to build a fire for warmth, but positioned himself on the rock bridge so that Zona and Nina could not leave the cliff overlooking the cascades. While picking up branches that had fallen on the rock ledge, for the purpose of making a fire, Zona had searched for a weapon but found none, not even a rock. It was an unintentional slip by Axel when he mentioned the bent gun barrel, but both girls had heard his words.

"How did you know that the gun barrel was bent?" asked Nina. Her first reaction was to pull back from the man. Axel had held her tightly and silently cursed himself for making the slip before learning where the canoe was hidden.

Axel protested that he had heard one or the other of the sisters mention it, but he knew that they didn't believe him. Nina said nothing more to indicate her suspicions, for she saw the man still controlled their escape path. Nina instead claimed that she couldn't remember where she and Zona had hidden the canoe and couldn't take Axel to it.

"You're fuckin' lying," accused Axel roughly.

"No, I'm not," denied the girl. Nina doubted her man. There was no way Axel could have known about the damaged gun unless he was at the spot where Yellow Fox died. She hoped that there was a logical explanation. Her shifting the location of the canoe to Zona was her way of stalling while she tried to figure it all out. Zona, she knew, would never reveal the location of the hidden craft. Nina stayed in Axel's arms and looked across the fire at Zona, hoping her sister could make sense for her out of all that was happening.

"The son-of-a-bitch that is holding you is married," her sister reminded her.

"Axel's wife is dead," replied Nina quietly.

A look of astonishment crossed Zona's face, "How do you know that?" she asked.

"I just know," said Nina, "Axel never really had a marriage. His wife took drugs. They hadn't lived together as husband and wife for months."

"I found out that Axel was married when his wife answered the telephone at his apartment," said Zona. "How did you find out?"

"Axel and I were with his wife the night that she died."

Nina's words were blunt but soft. "You were what?" Nina turned her head up to the man who was holding her.

"Tell Zona what happened," she said.

"She would never believe me," said the man. "You tell her."

"Axel's wife was taking drugs the night she died," began Nina. She spoke across the fire to her sister while Axel sat beside her and listened. "She called Axel when I was with him. Axel told me about her. I went with him to try to find her because she was saying crazy things to Axel over the telephone."

Nina saw the incredulous look on her sister's face, but continued.

"His wife worked in a laboratory out at the university in California when Axel and she were in school there. When they came to Minnesota, she got a job working in the laboratory at the college. She called Axel from the college laboratory when I was with him in his apartment, and Axel said she was taking some sort of drugs and was hallucinating. So we went over there, but the laboratory was locked up for the night and we couldn't get in. Axel pounded on the door, but nobody came. We went around to the windows where we could see into the basement where his wife worked. She was naked, stark naked. We could see her in there walking around. She didn't have a stitch of clothing on. We never did find her clothes that night."

Zona listened speechlessly.

"She was a tall woman," described Nina, "with thin legs and arms, and a body that tilted from side to side as she walked around the table waving a smoking glass flask like it was a champagne bottle. A single shock of faded brown hair, which she plaited, hung and bounced in the middle of her back. I remember she had a sprinkle of freckles on her nose, mostly below her eyes. They gave her an innocent look." Nina tried to remember the woman in the laboratory basement. "But she had a wonderful smile and hazel eyes. I thought she was the kind of person that would have a pleasant disposition."

"Even though she was married to Axel," Nina looked up at

the face of the man beside her, "I think that if I had gotten to know her, I would have liked her."

"We could see her through the bars on the basement window, but we couldn't get inside. She flopped down on the rubber mat that was on the floor. Axel said she probably had taken some LSD and that was what was making her act so crazy. We tried to get her attention by pounding on the window. She looked right at us but never did appear to know that we were there. She just sat there on the floor naked, holding the flask. Then almost as if making a toast, she threw back her head, opened her mouth, and poured the flask directly into her throat."

"She fell backwards as if struck by a blow and gagged. She appeared to try to scream, but the only sound we heard was the breaking of the flask. Her intake of breath caused her to choke, then she started vomiting and spewing the liquid into the air. It sprayed over her face and she clawed at her eyes and rolled on the floor. Her body jerked about on the floor in convulsions."

Nina looked at the man beside her. "Axel was like a wild man. We ran back around to the door, and he kicked in the glass, reached for the bar on the inside, and pulled it so that the door would come open. When we finally got to her, she was already dead. Axel wouldn't let me go near her. The liquid had burned her hair, her eyebrows, and even ate into the sockets of her eyes. Whatever she drank was some sort of a burning liquid. It charred away her face and most of her hair."

Zona stared at her sister in disbelief. "My God! The dead woman they found in our dormitory!"

Nina nodded. "Yes. Axel wrapped her in the rubber mat and carried her there."

"And, you weren't seen?" asked Zona.

Nina shrugged. "It was late. I went first and opened the doors and checked the hallways. No one saw us."

"Why our room?" asked Zona. "Why not the hospital? Why

didn't you call a doctor?"

"She was already dead, and Axel wanted to put her someplace where she wouldn't be found for awhile so that we could take his formula and get across the Canadian border."

"Why for God's sake?" asked Zona.

"Because the drug that Axel's wife had taken before she drank the acid was from one of the vials that contained the formula that Axel was taking to Lavel University."

"She wasn't taking LSD then like Axel claimed?" asked Zona.

"No," admitted Nina, "Axel said that taking the formula orally, the way his wife sampled it, had the same effect as a hallucinogen, like LSD, but it wasn't LSD."

"My God," Zona stared at the silent man who was letting her sister tell his tale, "what did you expect it would do to other people?"

"When injected into the muscles rather than the blood stream in smaller quantities, it doesn't have a hallucinogen effect," replied Nina.

"That's what Axel told you?" asked Zona.

"Yes, that's what Axel told me."

"You believed him?"

"Yes," said Nina.

"Why did you take her body to our dormitory?"

"It was in the same block as the laboratory," said Nina. "Where else could we have taken her? You had the car. We couldn't just call a taxi cab."

"So then you packed your suitcase and came to the lobby to get the car keys from me so you could drive to Canada, and I wouldn't let you go unless I went along."

Nina nodded.

"Christ," said Zona. "No wonder the police thought that it was me that was dead. Why did you put her in my bed? Why didn't you put her in your bed?"

Nina looked over at Axel. "We were both just so scared when he got her in the room that Axel just laid her in a bed and we locked the door. She smelled awful," commented Nina. "Did you know that when a person dies they lose all control of their body functions, and they just smell awful. It was probably because of the smell that the other girls in the dormitory found his wife's body before we could get across the Canadian border."

"And you pretended that you didn't know when we heard the radio broadcast, and you weren't going to tell me," accused Zona.

"What good would it do to involve you any more than I already had?" asked Nina. "I could think of nothing else to do. We should never have left her in the room, but when Axel said that was the only place we could take her body, I couldn't think of anywhere else to go. I was afraid one of the campus security guards would see us. When I heard the news report, I thought it was bad enough to have gotten you involved by leaving her body in our room."

"Why are you telling me now?" asked Zona.

Her sister trembled. "I've always thought that Axel is a good man, Zona, that's what I've really thought. He tried to save his wife from drinking that acid. I never thought he was the kind of man who could have killed our father."

While Nina was speaking, she slowly slipped her hand to the knife stuck in Axel Denek's waistband.

Zona dismissed her sister's words and spoke sudden, raw, and very angry words of her own. "I don't care what he tried to do for his wife. If I had Yellow Fox's knife, I would use it on him." Zona's bitter words were spoken directly to the man across the flickering fire.

Axel laughed and taunted Zona. "Do you really think that you could kill?" he asked with a grin. "Killing," he said, "takes talent. When you're going to kill with a knife, you have to turn the blade sideways so that it will slip in between the ribs and hit the heart. If you don't turn the blade, then it won't fit inside the rib cage, and the ribs will protect the vital organs. Do you think you can remember that?" he laughed aloud.

"And if you don't kill with your first thrust of the knife, then you don't get any more chances," he added. "After you stick it in between the ribs, then you've got to turn it a little because you got to let the blood out; got to hold it there while the heart drains out in your hand. That makes your hand slippery."

Axel laughed, "Just sticking it in, that ain't enough."

The man's gross description made Zona feel nauseated. She wanted to gag.

"Now," continued Axel, he was enjoying his torment, and he squeezed Nina's waist, "what your sister could do is take a knife and stick it in my stomach, but all that does is let loose the sour gasses. That won't stop a man from coming at you the way you can stop him when you put the point of the blade in his heart. You see, the heart's our center. When that blade point hits the heart, the shock just paralyzes."

"Now if I were to kill you," Axel Denek laughed, "I wouldn't go for your belly, I'd bury my knife underneath your left tit."

Zona shuddered, and Nina let her fingers brush against the hilt of the blade in Axel's waistband.

CHAPTER TWENTY-NINE

After Gary Faulks left his office, Errol Joyce sat at his desk and relived the ghastly kitchen scene that Marie Saulturs tearfully recounted for him that afternoon. Her telling of the events was so vivid, that in the darkness of his office, he saw it unfold in his mind.

Marie didn't scream at Anton. Her voice was low and deadly. "You're holding my children hostage. I don't care about me, but my girls will be ruined if you tell them that Tom Boushey is their father, that Tom and I have broken the taboo. They are good girls. God would not have given me such bright, intelligent children if what Tom and I did was bad. It is unfair for you to take advantage of what we did by threatening to hold the twins hostage."

Marie picked up the knife. It was a sharp filleting knife.

One Anton knew the woman used to carve up game and fish. She held it so that it was tightly against her chest, the blade pointed upward toward the ceiling.

In his drunkenness, Anton muttered, "You don't scare me with your knife. If you want Tom Boushey, go ahead." He threw his arms wide. "Carve my heart out."

Marie sobbed and looked at the blade in her hand. "The knife is not for you," she said.

She put her hand on the cutting board where she carved Anton's game. Laying the sharp blade across the finger that held the wedding ring that Anton Saulturs had given her in Chicago, she said, "I will pay you the Sioux ransom for the release of my daughters."

Anton Saulturs, through the fog of his befuddled mind, looked at the face of the woman and then focused his eyes on the hand. She had the knife pointed at the ring finger, poised to sever it from her hand. "You're joking," he said.

Marie shook her head, "No. You are holding my daughters hostage with your threats, just as sure as if you had them locked away. I will pay the Sioux ransom to you to buy your silence and to let me keep them. That way you will have your revenge, and I will have my daughters. You can take the ransom and get out of our lives."

Anton swayed on his feet and grinned. "Theatrics, Marie," he said. "You always were good with theatrics. You should have studied drama at the university rather than economics," and he grunted a laugh.

A bitter mask of hatred settled across Marie's face. She did not look at her hand. Instead she looked directly into his eyes and held him hypnotized as the blade slowly descended, and with a rocking motion, severed the finger on the cutting block as neatly as she disjointed game he brought home from the hunt.

In horror Anton watched the blood spurt.

Still looking into his eyes, as if in a trance, the mother curled the remaining fingers of the damaged hand into a fist and clutched the severed piece of bone and flesh. With an animal screech, she threw the bloody object at him. It struck his cheek with a smear, dropped, and went slithering across the floor.

Marie gagged, doubled over in pain, and grasped her damaged hand to her belly. Anton was shocked from his drunken stupor.

"My God!" he cried. The Indian grabbed a towel and seized the woman's hand to stop the flow of blood. But Marie took the towel and pushed him away. She wrapped it tightly around the stump on her hand, then again doubled over and sobbed.

Bewildered, Anton dropped on his knees to search for the severed finger. At that moment the kitchen door burst open and two little girls entered, calling for their dog. The two saw Marie bent over her hand that was clasped to her belly, and Anton was on the floor on his knees. The man shouted at the girls to leave.

"What have you done with our dog?" screamed Zona, looking about wildly at the blood.

"Get out!" roared Anton, and the two little girls fled.

In his office, Errol Joyce shuddered and shook his head in disbelief.

CHAPTER THIRTY

Nina wriggled against Alex Denek's warm body. She was intent on making the man aware of her presence. The campfire had become a bed of coals with occasional flickers that lighted Zona's face on the other side. As she shifted her hips to press against him, Nina's hand touched the silvered hilt of the knife at Axel's waist.

Zona looked across at her sister's display of affection. "Nina," she said, unable to contain her exasperation, "he isn't going to let us get out of here alive. He knows that I know he killed Yellow Fox, and he can't kill me unless he also kills you."

Nina bit her lip and did not reply.

Squeezing Nina again, Axel said, "Honey you know I love you." Nina kissed the cheek he lowered to her.

Zona spoke again, "Nina, this is the man who would have let Yellow Fox cut off your finger rather than admit he stole those paddles."

Axel turned to Zona and hissed, "You're the loving sister that tried to kill Nina."

Zona was struck speechless by the man's statement. Her eyes turned to the other woman.

Axel Denek continued, "Nina told me what happened."

"Axel, don't," pleaded Nina.

"Honey," said Axel, "we might just as well have this out now. That old Indian on the portage was a madman, but I knew he wouldn't cut off a woman's finger."

"You didn't know that," hissed Zona.

"You're telling your sister that I left her when the old Indian was threatening us with his knife and traps, but once you tried to kill your own sister by drowning her."

"It didn't happen that way," said Zona quietly.

"Oh, yes it did," said Axel. "Nina told me what happened." He repeated, "Tell her, Nina. Tell her what you told me."

Nina stopped her movement toward the knife. She again shook her head. "Axel, Don't," she repeated.

"Tell her," insisted Axel. "You know your sister pushed you off the ledge so that you would drown."

"That's not the way it happened," Zona said again. "We were only eight years old. That's not the way it happened."

For the moment, Nina forgot the knife at Axel's waist, and thought back over the years to their last encounter with their father. The twins had confronted their father in the kitchen of their home where they had gone looking for their dog that their father did not like and had threatened to destroy. Twice their dog had chewed on valuable furs their father had trapped.

The twins had entered the kitchen and smelled the sweet sickening odor of fresh blood. Their mother was standing at the kitchen cabinet, clutching her hand to her stomach, as if sickened by the sight of the gore on the floor. Their father was on his knees vomiting. Zona screamed that their father had butchered their little dog. Their father had shouted for them to leave, to get out of the kitchen. The sick man on the floor lifted his hands. Nina thought that he was going to strike them, but instead he shoved them toward the door. Their mother bent in her grief and choked.

The twins had left the scene that they did not understand and walked to the cliff overlooking the bay. Zona was beside herself with anger, accusing their father. Nina had tried to speak in his defense, and when she did, it simply made her eight-year-old sister more overwrought. Zona slapped at her sister. Nina had slapped her back, and Zona gave her a shove that pitched Nina backward off the cliff.

Both girls screamed in terror. Their father had come running out of the house and down to the bay barely in time to grasp the arm of Nina and pull her up on the ledge that she could not reach.

Anton held the limp form of Nina in his arms, and, in anger, accused Zona of purposely shoving her sister into the bay. Zona screamed back, accusing her father of killing their dog and at Nina for defending him. It was then that Zona said the thoughtless words that tore at Nina's heart. "I wish you had drowned!"

Nina had confided her story to her lover, Axel, never believing that he would repeat it as he had done, throwing into the face of Zona the accusation that she had tried to kill her twin.

"Why did you come to Duluth?" asked Nina innocently. Again the woman stealthily touched the hilt of the knife in the man's waistband.

"My wife was wanted on drug charges, so we left," he admitted with candor. "I chose the City of Duluth because I love the loons. My wife changed her name and got a job at the college lab doing clean-up work."

"No one was following to try to get your formula?" murmured Nina. He moved when her hand brushed his back above his belt. She paused, frozen. Her words were an attempt to keep his attention from her searching hand.

"No. That was just a convenient story," admitted Axel. "I really did that research work on the formula, and it's mine. If it works the way I think it will, I'll make a fortune."

From across the fire, Zona asked, "Don't you think the authorities will look for you in Canada?"

As her sister held the man's attention, Nina touched the cold blade and traced it with her fingers to feel if it was held to the man's waist by anything other than his belt.

"I'm an expert at running," replied Denek, with a laugh. "I learned that when I was a kid on the streets of Los Angeles. There's lots of names a man can use and lots of places he can go."

"When you get the canoe back, you're going to kill us, aren't you?" said Zona quietly. Axel felt Nina stiffen involuntarily at his side when her sister spoke. He grasped her tightly, and felt the girl twist at his waist. "Why do you say that?" he evaded.

"You are, aren't you?" insisted Zona. The girl looked at her sister rather than the man. Nina's eyes had a strange look Zona thought, as if her concentration was somewhere other than at their campfire.

Nina's thoughts were at another place, for at that moment she felt the knife slip from Axel's waistband into the palm of her hand. The twin had successfully relieved the man of the weapon by her charade of affectionate touching. Nina thought her breathing would betray her and she remained still to see if Axel noticed before again moving her hand and getting a firm grip on the handle of the blade.

"You think evil thoughts," Axel said with a grin.

Concealing the knife within her folded arms, Nina untangled herself from the man beside her and sat up straight. She looked directly into Axel's eyes, and to his surprise quietly asked, "Did you kill my father?"

"Nina," whined Axel, reaching out for her again.

The twin drew away. "You knew about the gun," she said

softly, "so you must have been there where my father died."

From across the fire, Zona saw her sister's move. She, too, had been taken by surprise when her twin abruptly turned on her lover. Zona steeled herself to be ready to leap.

"Goddamn it, Nina, where's the fuckin' canoe?" The mask of pretense was completely gone from Axel's face.

"You did kill him, didn't you?" insisted the girl.

"Yes," hissed Axel. "I've had enough of the games you two are playing. Tell me where you have hidden that canoe!"

Without taking her eyes off of the man, Nina called across the campfire to her sister, "You were right all along, Zona, he is a son-of-a-bitch."

Zona gathered her legs under her preparing to spring, for she saw the knife flash in Nina's hand at the same instant that Axel slapped at this waistband and discovered it missing.

With a roar, Axel rolled to his knees and grabbed for Nina. Zona leaped across the fire, but Axel deflected her body with a blow to her face that sent her rolling to the edge of the ledge. As Axel turned again to Nina, he felt an explosion in his chest. As he fell against the girl, he heard Nina's words murmur through gritted teeth, "Turn the blade, twist, and let the blood out."

Axel Denek fell back to the ground. His eyes glazed. The last mortal sight that they registered was an evening star twinkling down at him through the forest's canopy. The smell of death rose from him and spread across the campsite.

CHAPTER THIRTY-ONE

The early moon cast a ghostly light through the trees and lit up the clearing. Zona and Nina sat on the same log where they encountered Yellow Fox, where the Indian had made them sit and spread their fingers. Neither girl could stand the sight and smell of Axel's dead body. Zona stomped out the fire on the rocks, and the girls carefully made their way in the faint light to the clearing on the portage to await the dawn.

"Oh God! We're both covered with blood," breathed Nina. The blood from the blow to Zona's face had stopped flowing, but it had caked on her breasts where it ran inside her jacket. Nina's jacket sleeve was soaked with the dead man's blood. There was also a spot on Nina's thigh where she had wiped Axel's blood from the blade of the knife. "It belongs to us," explained Nina tersely when she thrust the cleaned blade into her waistband.

The scratches on Zona's face and head attracted swarms of mosquitoes. Nina's own body ached at every joint and muscle.

"Zona," asked Nina after a long silence. "When we were little, did you really try to drown me when you pushed me off the cliff?"

By the light of the moon, Zona looked into Nina's eyes. She thought she saw something very new and fragile. "Do you know that in all these years you never asked me? You just assumed the worst. You never asked me." Zona's voice was almost bitter.

"I'm asking now," said Nina quietly. "I was in that water for a long time. I couldn't reach the ledge. I was so scared. I didn't think our father was going to be able to hold on to me. I looked up and saw your face at the edge of the bluff looking down at me. I didn't want to believe that you did it on purpose."

Zona compressed her lips and shook her head. "You pushed at me and I just pushed back," she said. "I didn't mean for you to slip and fall off." She looked at her sister. Tears glistened in her eyes. "I've always loved you, Nina, but after that you made me stay at arms length when we played, when we were in school, and when we were growing up - you always kept me at arms length."

"I guess," whispered Nina, "I did that because I was afraid. Father said you pushed me off the cliff on purpose."

"Our father was wrong," said Zona bitterly. "That's why I hated him. He never came back to tell you that he was wrong. He was the one who kept you from really being my sister all those years while we were growing up together. I don't wish Yellow Fox to be dead, but I'm glad I don't have to see him or have to talk to him again. For me, the day he took my sister away from me was the day he stopped being my father."

Nina turned on the log and put her arms around Zona. The two girls grasped each other and sobbed.

"The real reason I almost drowned," choked Nina, "was that I saw blood on father's sleeve and on the back of his hand when he reached for me. At first I wouldn't take his hand. His face was there above me, telling me to grab his hand, but I could see the blood. He saw why I wouldn't reach out for him because he pulled back that arm and reached out with his other arm and caught me."

Nina wiped her face with the sleeve of her jacket. "Later, when we were in the house, I thought maybe I was just imagining I saw blood on his shirt sleeve, but while mother stood in the doorway with her hand to her stomach and crying, I saw our father roll up his sleeve to hide the blood. Mother never came near me," she added.

Zona stared at her sister. "And all these years you thought that I shoved you off the bluff on purpose to try to drown you, and you thought that father killed our dog, even though you didn't want to believe me when I told you he had, and you thought mother didn't love you because she didn't come near you that day? She let father put you to bed before he left our home."

Nina nodded. "Yes."

"All these years," said Zona, "you didn't think that any of us loved you?"

Nina shook her head. "Not really. I think I would have run away then, but I had no place to go. Mother was sick the next day. She didn't come near me; she didn't come near me for several days because she was sick. She just kept holding her hand to her stomach and avoiding me, except to bring some soup."

"And you didn't want to see me?" reminded Zona.

"Yes."

"And you thought father killed our dog and left when he found out that you saw the blood on his sleeve?" added Zona.

"Yes." Then her lip trembled. "I didn't want to believe it Zona. I loved him." Zona patted Nina's arm. "I know, you always did," she replied.

Zona led her sister to a flat rock with a back ledge for them to lean against. Before they dropped into exhausted sleep, Zona put her arms around her sister and held her. She whispered, "I'm sorry about Axel, and I'm sorry about our father, Nina."

Nina sobbed.

The twins lay on the rock and were asleep in each other's arms when the Indian schoolteacher, Tom Boushey, found them.

CHAPTER THIRTY-TWO

The funeral service for Yellow Fox, Anton Saulturs, the professor from the tribe of the Saskatchewan Ojibwa, the hunter, the trapper, and the gatherer of wild rice, took place on the reservation burial ground within sound of the trucks and cars that sped over U.S. Highway 61 on their way between Fort William in Ontario, Canada and Duluth, Minnesota.

The highway was close enough to the old cemetery that the noise made it difficult to hear, and the pounding of the wheels caused older tombstones to lean out of plumb because there was not enough topsoil to set them properly. Most of the old graves, Errol Joyce noted, were underground, but many were crypts that stuck out above the surface and rested on solid bedrock. The crowd waded through damp undergrowth that surrounded the graves, covered with the dew left when morning daybreak covered the hill with purple mist.

P.M. Gregory was there, as was Jan Kiel, Marie Saulturs, and her three daughters. Tom Boushey and Engel Tormudson had come. The two visitors from Washington, D.C., Ivella Zahn and Alejandro Doman, had stayed over to attend the service. Judge Clemens and her fat reporter arrived in the same car. Peter Hauck and his personal secretary, Terry Whitehall-Banning, again in a stunning outfit, stood at the edge of the crowd. Two hundred Indians crowded onto the small cemetery grounds.

The coffin rested on two-by-fours that spanned the gaping grave. Later the lumber would be removed, and the coffin would be lowered to its final resting place. The simple wooden container was nailed tightly shut. Three Medicine Men of the tribe clustered at one end of the coffin. Marie and her children stood at the other.

They all waited.

Errol Joyce and P.M. Gregory were standing far enough to the back that almost everyone was in their line of sight. Up on the hill away from the crowd, tom-tom beaters took turns striking a large stretched skin that gave forth a deep monotonous rumble. Each beat of the drum was followed by an interval of silence that Errol estimated to be about three seconds long. The drum had been sending out its throbbing echoes since before Errol and P.M. arrived, and the two men had been there fully a half-hour. There was no indication that the beaters intended to stop.

Someone had laid the dead man's yellow fur on top of the casket. It had been brushed and combed.

Errol looked at the somber face of Engel Tormudson. The tall, thin, cadaverous Indian stood straight as a ramrod. His arms folded, his eyes fastened on the coffin.

Dorothy Clemens had been surprised by Marie Saulturs' withdrawal of her defense. That very morning the judge entered judgment in favor of Engel Tormudson, who was now assured that he would be the next chief and chairman of the tribal council. Not without complication, Errol thought. The lawyer had received a telephone call from New York, which indicated that Engel was already having trouble doing the refinancing that he promised the judge that he would obtain.

The three daughters of Marie Saulturs huddled around their mother, protecting her. Errol thought that he should have guessed that the three would stand with their mother who they dearly loved. He had heard that the twins intended to transfer to the university campus in Minneapolis and that Marie intended to take her youngest daughter and move there. The chief had announced her resignation. If any of the tribe regretted her leaving, none of the regret showed in the stoic faces of the Ojibwa that surrounded her, her daughters, and the coffin of Anton Saulturs.

Errol had spoken to the police officer in Duluth. The man admitted that he had no evidence that would implicate Nina in removing the body of the naked woman from the laboratory where she died, and he said that he did not intend to search for any. The Cook County Sheriff agreed with Joyce that the killing of Axel Denek was justifiable homicide. Nina and Zona maintained that they forgot where they concealed the canoe that contained Axel Denek's formula. P.M. Gregory's canoe was never recovered, but mysteriously, on the morning of the funeral, a new eighteen-foot Alumnacraft appeared on his lawn.

Errol Joyce watched Jan Kiel awkwardly ease her bulky figure through the crowd of Indians bunched below the great drum. She moved behind Zona Saulturs. Zona turned and clasped her friend in her arms. They clung to each other for only a fraction of the drumbeats but long enough for a whispered exchange of words.

"I am sorry for Anton's death, but I am happy you and Nina have made up," breathed Jan.

Zona gently patted her friend's swollen belly. As she did so, she nodded toward the two men standing on high ground on the edge of the crowd. "Have you and Errol made up?" she asked. There was not time for more words. Jan stepped back, for Nina waved to her and then indicated over Zona's shoulder for Jan to send her to an indicated place beside her younger sister and mother. Jan did so and stepped around Tom Boushey. She acknowledged his presence. Then, turning her back on the site of the grave, she started walking to the high ground on the far side of the small cemetery.

She stopped where Errol Joyce and P.M. Gregory were standing. Without a word, she turned and slipped her hand into Errol's. He glanced down at her, but the woman lawyer wasn't looking at him. Her attention was on the twins. With their little sister, they stood at the end of the wood coffin holding hands, as if to surround and protect their mother.

Jan Kiel spoke so softly, Errol could barely hear her words. "Think of what those two girls have missed while growing up," breathed Jan, "just because each girl thought something that happened in their life was true, when it wasn't. They were so positive about what they thought they knew about their own mother, about their real father, and about their mother's husband. Jesus! They lost so much when they were eight years old and made that mistake."

Tears welled in Jan Kiel's eyes. She squeezed his hand tighter. "And I have lost so much these past months." She looked up at the tall lawyer. "Do you think we could start all over again?" she asked.

P.M. Gregory pretended not to notice, but out of the corner of his eye, he saw his friend pull Jan closer to his side. He heard the soft answer. "Yes," said Joyce. "I think we can."

Tom Boushey stood behind Marie and her family. Tom had admitted to Errol that he was still overwhelmed by the knowledge that he was the father of the twins that he had always dearly loved. It would take him some time to get used to parenthood, he confided.

The drum on the hill stopped.

The Medicine Man, who appeared to be the eldest of the three, began to speak. Errol had attended Ojibwa funerals before. He held Jan's hand, and with head bowed, listened to hear the words of the mighty Menaboju, the Indian's favorite demi-god, who is never named in Ojibwa religious ceremonies, but who is always there:

"The soul of life travels in a fragile canoe - light, tough, supple, mysterious, and magic-like the yellow leaf in autumn. Like the yellow water-lily carried over turbulent and calm waters until, finally, it sinks back into eternity; there to be renewed, and with its soul, set afloat again, and again, and again."

THE END